Praise For *The Saga of Baldar and Brithwynn*

"This story is so intense! Sophie, you are so talented!!!!! Loved being able to have this from you. You're truly amazing."
- April Cox

"Great story so far. Love it!!!"
- Christopher Lizon

"Good stuff... you do know how to write a compelling story good lady!"
- Alex Cooley

"Awesome!"
- Jeanne Stanley

"This is truly a good tale."
- Valeree Hicks

"And please allow me to say how awesome this is!"
- B. Scott Dickson

Also by Sophie G. Michaels

"Return to Bethlehem"
In *An Atlas to Time, Space, and Bonfires*

"The Battle of Anderida Forest"
In *The Odds are Against Us*

While Rivers Flow

THE SAGA OF BALDAR AND BRITHWYNN

THE SAGA OF BALDAR AND BRITHWYNN

SOPHIE G. MICHAELS

Artelune Publishing

The Saga of Baldar and Brithwynn

Published by Artelune Publishing
Tampa, Florida
For information on this book or any of our other
titles, please contact the Director of Sales at
407-209-6494.

ISBN 979-8-9896290-2-2 (paperback)
ISBN 979-8-9896290-3-9 (ebook)

10 9 8 7 6 5 4 3 2 1

First Artelune Trade Paperback Edition: December
2024

Printed in the United States of America

Cover art and design by Grace Schosser

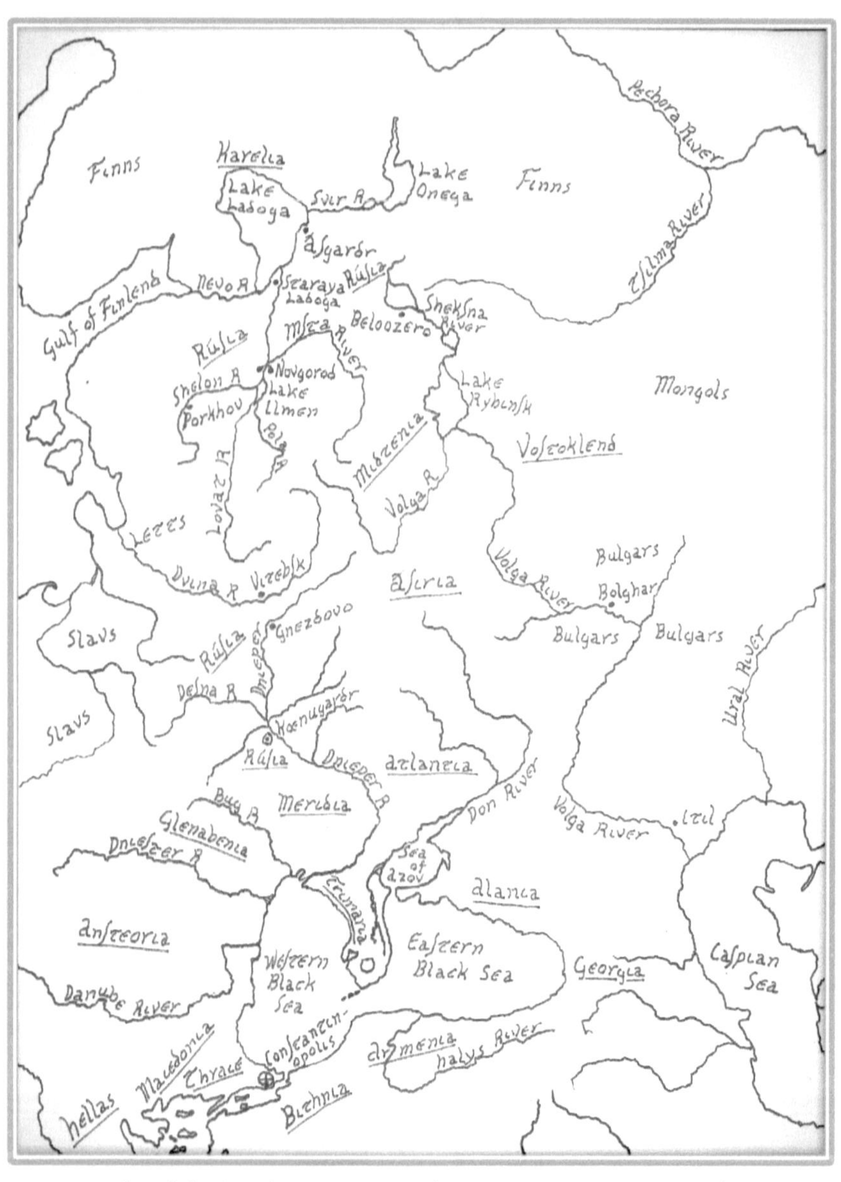

The Rús lands and eastern Bysantinsk Empire, circa 6621 Anno Mundi

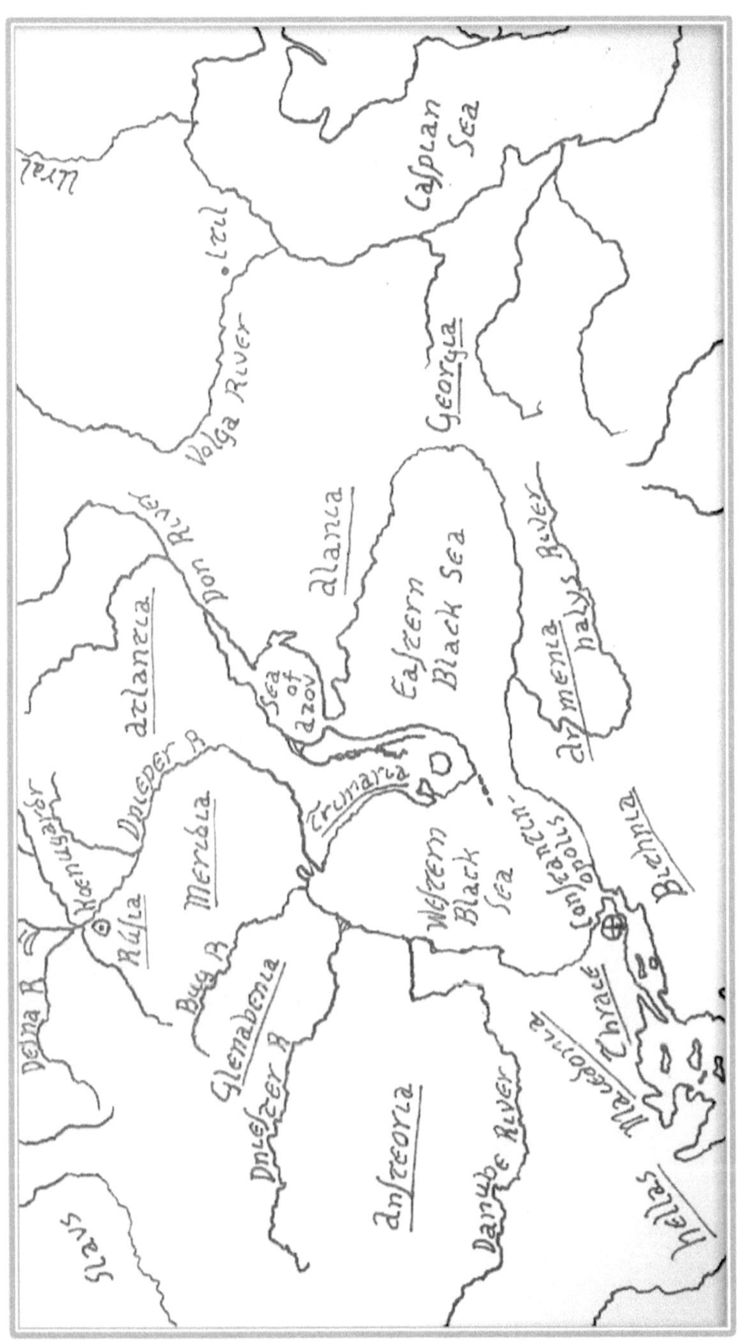

The northeastern Bysantinsk Empire, circa 6621 Anno Mundi

The Bysantinsk kingdom of Trimaria, circa 6621 Anno Mundi

For Alex, who asked me to write a short story for him and didn't complain when it grew,
For April, who proved to be the heroine I needed,
For those we lost along the way,
And for everyone who volunteered to populate Trimaria.
May you live forever amid the warm sands of my homeland.

Contents

Preface

"Write the story of our reign, as if it took place back in the Middle Ages."

It was an appealing challenge, and one that I was honored to accept.

If you've ever participated in Living History or Reenactment in general, you may have noticed that it can take a certain amount of creativity to maintain the "magic" of the reenactment, despite inescapable mundanities and the limited size of the event. It's just something we learn to live with, a reminder that this is just a game.

But what if there were no limitations? What if you could follow the action to any part of the world you wanted and the only modernisms were the ones you *chose* to include? What if you could include your fellow reenactors in all the twists and turns of your plot, regardless of whether they could or would behave like that in real life? Regardless of whether it would get half of them killed?

What if it were a book?

I was greatly honored to be asked to write the story of this reign, and even more honored that so many of my fellow reenactors were willing to have me name characters after them.

We lost many friends that year, or at least that's how it seemed. Some losses were expected, some were a shock to all of us. And one, a close friend, read this work in her hospital bed as she was being treated for cancer. I'll never forget trying not to cry with her as I watched her read about her character. This book gave me the opportunity to keep her alive and vibrant, the way she's supposed to be. The way they're all supposed to be.

This work is dedicated to all those Trimarians, past, present, and future, who inspired it. I hope you'll enjoy reading this work as much as

I enjoyed writing it. May you live forever amid the warm sands of my homeland.*

* This line borrowed shamelessly from Mistress Warjna Waleska Kaztjmjr of the SCA kingdom of Trimaris, with her kind permission.

I

Porphyrogénita

"Come away, Princess!" Valgarðr, the head of her personal guard, hissed again. "There's no time now for mourning!"

Brithwynn hardly heard him. Her beloved father lay stretched out on the grand imperial bed, the gold and purple silk straightened and tidied by the quietest of the servants after his agonies ended. The Patriarch and a few other members of the Court had been and gone, each done with her father now that power had passed from him to – whom?

Her half-brother Ióannés, most likely. He was the eldest son born after their father came to the throne, the first heir born in this very room, where all legitimate children of a sitting emperor began their lives. His status as Sebastokrator had grown ever since he first led the armies of the Empire against its enemies as a dew-faced young man, strengthening the Empire's position in the lands to the north of the Black Sea, where the semi-autonomous kingdoms of Ansteoria, Glenabenia, Meridia, and Atlantia were under continued assault by barbarian tribes, and continuing the Mediterranean gains that had begun two centuries earlier during the reign of Constantine VII until it included more of the ancient Empire than it had under even the great Augoustos Justinian. The Empire now stretched east nearly to the Caspian Sea, west to include parts of Italia, north to the borders of the Kievan Rús, and south to Aegyptus and part of Arabia.

And yet this heroic prince and heir presumptive of the Basileia tôn Rhōmaiōn was one to be avoided, for his glance was death to any he considered an enemy. It was whispered that he was behind the deaths of three of their cousins and two of Brithwynn's older brothers. She could think of none other likely to have both the power and drive to eliminate them.

There were plenty of others who lusted after her father's power, though. Her stepmother Maria was rumored to want the path to the throne cleared of heirs from Alexios' two prior marriages so one of her young sons could claim the Throne of Solomon. Her brother Isaak had only recently reached majority but now fought for the greatness Ióannés had already achieved. Her half-sister Euphrosyne had been married off to the basilios of Georgia as much to stop her scheming for the throne as to bring the small and distant kingdom under the Aegis Rhōmaiōn, but now she could use that power base to become Augousta of all Rhōmania. Several of her uncles and cousins had retired to their personal estates when Alexios fell ill, either to guard themselves against assassination or to marshal their forces in a bid for the throne.

"Princess! We must leave!" Valgarðr grew more agitated. "It's no longer safe for you here."

"Leave?" The word cut through Brithwynn's grief, causing her to turn and stare at the Varangian. "How can I leave my father's side, or his palace?"

"It's no longer your father's palace, Princess!" he hissed again, with an uncertain glance back toward where his men guarded the entrance to the room and the passage beyond. "Do you want to die like him?"

"But!" she sputtered. She knew as well as any that Death stalked the halls of the Blachernai Palace, seeking out unsuspecting wearers of the imperial purple, especially the porphyrogénnēti like herself who were born to it.

"Farewell, Papa," she said, tears falling uncontrollably as she rose from her knees and kissed her father on the cheek. She glided from the Purple Chamber, escorted silently by Valgarðr and the rest of her Varangians. In her hands, she clutched the silk and gold embroidered cloth she had used to mop her father's brow through his last days.

* * *

Her ladies had known – or guessed – that Brithwynn had to leave the palace now that the emperor was dead. The fifteen of them already wore simple grey robes instead of their bright court gowns. They looked like... like the quiet servants who even now stood against the walls of her chamber or packed up the contents of her room. Her massive chests sat empty or well-rummaged, their contents stuffed into simple leather bags and packages. As she stood there, uncertain, Eirene and Theadora began closing the chests, locking some to disguise the fact that they'd been emptied.

"Let's get you changed, Highness," Verina said, guiding her to one side of her room, where her ladies held out their pallas to shield her from the guards' eyes. "We've got everything else ready." She and Ariadne slipped Brithwynn's red silk court gown off of her and replaced it with an unremarkable grey gown. The dark wool matched her mood, though it did nothing to alleviate the chill in her bones.

"If you're ready?" Valgarðr asked, as her ladies parted.

How dare he! Brithwynn thought. It was horrible enough that she had to leave her father's palace, the place she had always called home, but to be hurried along by the crude Varangian her father had entrusted her safety to! Unspeakable!

Her safety. The thought stopped her cold. Papa had been murdered by a member of their own family, someone who wouldn't have a problem killing her too. Valgarðr was right to hustle her along.

"How do we get out of here?" she asked, swallowing her pride and picking up one of the bags. It was quite heavy, but she tried not to let the surprising weight affect her well-schooled demeanor.

Her ladies rushed to follow her example. A part of Brithwynn's mind calmly noted that many of her ladies were equally surprised by the bags' weight.

"You and your ladies need to pass as servants," Valgarðr commanded. "They're invisible and go everywhere. You're in small groups going to servants' quarters or the kitchens, we're nearby going to barracks or to see our girlfriends among the maids. Nobody watches the servants' quarters. We can get out from there."

"And then?"

"Let me get you out of the palace first, Princess. For now, just trust me."

Huzzah. Her life was in the hands of a guardsman who probably had no clue how he was going to get her to safety.

* * *

"You three should go now," Valgarðr said to Brithwynn and the two ladies who would escort her to the servants' quarters. Verina and Theadora had taken down her elegant hairstyle and replaced it with a simple servant's chignon. "Stay with Metrodora and try to act like her. My men will be close."

Brithwynn hefted the lighter bundle one of the servants had replaced her original bag with. She allowed herself a tight grimace before carefully modeling Metrodora's slumped shoulders and downcast gaze.

Verina took the heavy door's handle and held it open, bracing herself against it as if she were accustomed to holding it open while toting a big bundle of dirty laundry. She held it open long enough for the other three women to pass through with their burdens, then released it with a loud sigh.

Brithwynn had to stop herself from turning to check on Verina, realizing just in time that the older woman had simply been trying to appear more believable as an old maidservant.

She would have to make herself as believable.

Before they'd turned down five passages, Brithwynn found she was completely lost. They were into the passageways used by the palace servants, smaller and darker than any the Family ever used. Rough stones replaced the smooth marble Brithwynn had always trod. Torches set into the walls were many orguiáe apart, far enough apart that the circle of light from one barely reached to the next one.

They could be following a passage into Hell itself, save that there was no smell of sulphur or screams of agony from the tormented.

Brithwynn crossed herself.

A few more orguiáe, and a trio of palace guards turned the corner ahead of them. Brithwynn stiffened in fear and almost dropped her bundle, suddenly certain that they had already been caught.

In the moment before she could get her legs to move, certain it was already too late, she recognized the swaggering guard who winked boldly at her. Kormákr would never have dared do so if she were not passing as a servant.

Brithwynn caught her breath, and the Varangian smiled. Reassuringly?

Beside her, Theadora gave her free hand a light squeeze before shifting her burden to her hip and smiling up at the trio of sturdy warriors.

"Haven't you boys got something better to do than make eyes at the new girl?" she asked.

The Varangians stuttered replies that made no sense to Brithwynn, though she got the impression that they would have said something more... *comprehensible* if they hadn't been concerned about offending her royal sensibilities.

Instead, they hustled off down the hall toward the group of Varangians Brithwynn knew kept pace behind her seven or eight orguiáe, and Metrodora started forward again toward the maids' rooms and the relative security that lay within

* * *

"Now what do we do?" young Thekla asked plaintively, as the women gathered in the small chamber where Metrodora and her fellow maidservants slept.

"We rest," Verina answered, patting her on the shoulder. "It will be some time before the rest of our group arrives, and we can do nothing until then. Besides, it may be some time before we can rest as securely."

The girl hardly seemed to believe her, but she curled up obediently on one of the pallets despite her doubts. Brithwynn found a pallet as well, knowing she must be a good example and that the next few days might be nearly as tiring as the previous week had been.

Before she knew it, Brithwynn was asleep.

She woke to find the room much more crowded than before. Her ladies lay sleeping or were just waking, and the Varangians crowded the space between them and the door. Niphon sat cross-legged in a small space between Brithwynn's mat and the one beside her, where Catella still slept.

"Princess, you're awake," Valgarðr said, noticing her almost immediately and stepping toward her as quickly as he could in the crowded chamber. "Very good – we're ready now. Servants start the day early, and we want to be out of the palace before anyone wearing gold starts to stir."

"How?" she asked, getting her feet under her and rising. She felt unexpectedly stiff and sore, certainly from sleeping on such a hard mat.

"The same way we got here," he said. "Servants come and go from the palace all the time. We take bundles and carts out into the city and get lost in the crowds."

Lost indeed! She would be lost as soon as she passed out of sight of the Palace, sooner if she couldn't recognize it from outside.

"And where do we go from here?"

"We leave the palace in small groups, Princess," Valgarðr replied. "We go into the city, inside the Wall of Constantine, and make our way to the ferries that ply the Chrysókeras. Then we cross to the north side and press on far from here."

"We are *within sight* of the Theodosian walls and escape: why would we go deeper into the city?" Thalassia demanded.

"We are," Verina told her, "but we might never reach them if we attempt that route. The sixth and seventh hills are far more open than the rest of the City. If you were watching – and someone is surely watching, if not *specifically* for our princess – what would you think if a large number of servants and men left the Blachernae and immediately turned toward one of the city gates?"

"Oh," Thalassia seemed surprised. Brithwynn felt her skin grow cold at the thought of how easily they might have fallen into such a simple trap.

"Good," Valgarðr said. "Wake the rest of your women, so we can go."

Brithwynn turned to wake Catella, her glance falling on Niphon. She was pleased to see her father's favorite scribe one last time before they left, though she was surprised that the young Egyptian would risk getting caught up in her troubles.

"Good Niphon, why are you here among my sad exiles?" she asked. "Should you not be with the other scribes, where you can claim ignorance of our doings?"

"I cannot, Highness," he answered miserably.

"Niphon is too well known as your father's personal scribe," Ismenia explained. "He has written correspondences that claimants to the throne would kill to destroy or have made public. Moreover, his script is recognizable to any who have read your father's edicts and missives. It would be exactly what a pretender needs to make a false will naming them as Heir, and no one can withstand the tortures that would be used on him to force his hand. He must come with us or die, and your father would have preferred for him to flee with us."

"Niphon! This is true?" she asked, horrified.

"Yes, Highness," he replied, bowing flat against the floor from his seated position. "I cannot ask this, but I beg that I might join you."

"You are most welcome, my friend," Brithwynn said, taking his hands in hers. "Both for your sake and for my father's."

Tears spilled over Niphon's growing smile.

* * *

Brithwynn shivered in the cool morning air. The steep hillside outside the Blachernae made her feel terribly exposed, though few people were outside this early in the morning.

That, perhaps, was one reason why she felt so exposed. The other reasons were that the area was far more open than any part of the Blachernae grounds had been. And that she knew someone was seeking her, or would be soon. That alone could make a person feel exposed.

Verina chivvied her toward the more populous quarter of the city between the fifth hill and the Constantinian Wall. Soon enough, the busier and more enclosed spaces helped her feel a little more at ease, though she continued to try watching for signs of danger.

Valgarðr's men surrounded them in a loose web, never so close that a spying eye should be able to see anything out of the ordinary. Somewhere, too, her other ladies walked with the maids whose knowledge of the City made them a blessing in the unfamiliar streets. The knowledge made Brithwynn feel more secure, though she'd give almost anything to be safely ensconced in whatever palace Valgarðr was taking her to.

They finally made it to the open gate in the Constantinian Wall and passed through without incident, taking the next street to the north-east and the minor gate of Eis Pegas, where fishermen and merchants crowded the area. Again, the guards seemed to take no special notice of them, though Brithwynn's heart was in her throat the entire time. Verina and the maid Passara seemed unfazed by their danger and were able to chat easily with the young guardsman, who called Verina "mother."

Brithwynn had often looked down on the broad waterway known as the Chrysókeras from high in the Blachernae Palace, but it seemed wider up close. And more... *fragrant*, despite its mirror-like gleam in the early morning sun. Fishwives hawked their men's morning catches, adding to the shore area's strong mélange of aromas.

Verina led the way here to a distant dock, where a small ferry boat waited. Nearby, Brithwynn noticed several of her Varangians, though now they wore the everyday clothes of Constantinopolis's regular citizens. The sight made her feel much more secure.

Verina led her and Passara straight to a small ferry boat, one that had seen many years' use transporting commoners across the Chrysókeras. In its small shelter, four of her ladies and two of her maids waited, their eyes wide with fear as they looked toward Brithwynn and the two who accompanied her.

Brithwynn stepped forward to join them, though she quailed as the boat shifted in the small waves at the dock. More gingerly, she continued to the far side of the shelter and squeezed in beside Zephrina and Juliana. They moved over, giving her more than enough room. Verina sat on the bench near Theadora, while Passara took a seat on the floor with the other maids.

The other women reached the ferry in twos and threes, followed shortly by the Varangians. The boat's small crew untied it almost immediately and rowed it out into the Chrysókeras, ignoring their passengers as they moved among other ferries, ships from across the Empire, and the ubiquitous fishing vessels. The breeze rose as they reached open water, and Brithwynn felt as if she could suddenly breathe again.

The boat's crew must have been well paid to leave when it was less than half full and to row so steadily for the less-populated north shore. Brithwynn could only hope it had been her father's people who had paid them so highly – and that they hadn't been outbid or changed sides. If they had, her freedom would certainly end within moments of their arrival. Her life, too, along with the freedom and probably the lives of many of her companions.

She could only hope that Valgarðr's apparent calm was well-founded.

Nobody had met them at the docks, nor had anyone stopped them from reaching the small private dwelling just inside the walls where they now awaited Valgarðr's return. Brithwynn tried to swallow another bite of the bread the housewife had offered them, but her mouth was too dry. A swallow of wine helped, though the vintage was barely better than vinegar.

The outer door burst open. Brithwynn jumped, knowing as she did that it was probably Valgarðr. She and the ladies who waited with her exchanged frightened glances, though she managed to keep herself from sighing with relief the way most of them did.

"Well?" she asked, as Valgarðr appeared in the doorway.

"Everything is ready," he said, offering the merest bob of his head as a bow. Outside, he hadn't even done that. It had been a shock to Brithwynn the first time she saw him ignore all courtly rules of conduct, but it also convinced her that he took his duty seriously. He would never willingly do anything to reveal her to her enemies, certainly nothing as unnecessary as following the little niceties of behavior appropriate to the royal court.

"I need to talk with you and Verina alone," Valgarðr said. "Can you…"

A wave of her hand, and her ladies left for the house's small courtyard, which the homeowners had already slipped off to.

Valgarðr gingerly sat on the second stool beside the rickety old table where Brithwynn was already seated. "So many of your nobles have suddenly decided to visit their home estates for a while, I've been able to get ahold of carriages belonging to some of your lesser nobles. One of your ladies – Ismenia, I think – will take a large escort and go to the Tagaris estate before meeting us later. Lady Verina will leave as a Maliasene and head into Macedonia, where their estate is. You'll be one of Verina's women. Everyone else will travel the whole way as common folk, so it'll take longer for them to catch up."

"So we're going to Maliasenos lands?" Brithwynn asked. "I didn't know they were powerful enough to offer any protection."

She'd barely known that family existed.

Valgarðr shifted on the shaky old stool.

"They aren't," he finally said. "They're only unimportant enough to make you invisible till we get far from the capital."

"So we're hiding in Macedonia?" she asked.

"Not exactly," he said.

"But what's beyond Macedonia?" Brithwynn asked in annoyance, though a part of her realized that Valgarðr was withholding information not to torment her but to protect her from the spies who might even now be listening. Walls had ears, as did even the most innocent-looking of objects. "It's practically the edge of the Empire!"

"Not quite."

Brithwynn looked with disbelief at her two most trusted supporters. Where on earth could they be taking her?

"Your safety lies in the distant reaches of the Empire," Verina said. "Your father planned for this."

* * *

Brithwynn wished, not for the first time, that she could travel openly. The wayhouses Valgarðr insisted on choosing were barely suitable for the poor noblewoman Verina pretended to be and would never have been chosen if she had been traveling openly. Even here, Valgarðr insisted that they take tables in darkened corners and dreary rooms, where the wind sought entry and made lamps gutter. On nights like this, the wool gowns she and her ladies wore stopped most of the cold and rain but had taken on the strong aroma of wet sheep.

If she had traveled openly as herself, the greatest nobles of the provinces would have vied for the honor of hosting her. She would have been feasted in warm, well-lit halls and lounged on dry cushions while wearing silks and pearls.

Unless they so feared being attacked by a more powerful claimant to the Throne that they shunned her or turned her over to one of them in exchange for protection. Then she would be worse off than she was now.

With that pleasant thought in mind, Brithwynn had even more trouble than usual stomaching the ubiquitous watery bean soup, whose only meat content was the questionably-sourced grease that topped it. It seemed to be the specialty of all the wayhouses Valgarðr had found for them thus far.

She prayed that nobody outside their small party could tell how little she – or anyone but the Varangians, who could eat anything – had managed to eat. She played with her food, pretending to eat it. A few more minutes, and she could pass her bowl to one of them and act like she had eaten something.

Brithwynn looked up when the door swung open, making all but a few of the lamps go out and the fire sputter in its brazier. She immediately dropped her eyes to her bowl but listened intently as their fellow travelers reacted to the unexpected arrival of the two new travelers.

Many yelled or grumbled threateningly, while some stood and took up the weapons they kept close.

Whether because they knew they risked being set upon by their fellow travelers or to keep out the cold driving rain that must have soaked them thoroughly, the two men at the door shut it firmly the moment they were through. Most of their fellow travelers settled grumbling back onto their benches or went to the brazier with a straw to relight their table lamps, though a few chose to draw sharpening stones as an excuse to keep their weapons out.

The two newcomers made their way directly toward the open table closest to the brazier, pulling back their rain-slicked cloaks and dropping them on the benches beside them. Their wool tunics looked clean and well-made in comparison with everyone else in the wayhouse, making Brithwynn feel every long day that had passed since she last took a real bath or wore clothes that were truly clean. They stood out amid their grungy surroundings and fellow travelers.

Brithwynn couldn't help feeling that they didn't belong.

Several of the other travelers in the small room must have had the same idea, moving back from the newcomers' table. More than one slipped out the narrow, curtained doorway leading upstairs to the wayhouse's small guest chambers.

Brithwynn was just beginning to fantasize about moving to one of the newly-vacated tables a little closer to the small fire when Valgarðr caught her eye. He shook his head minutely, then gestured with his thumb toward the ragged curtain.

Huzzah. It was time to retire to the sty they called a room.

* * *

"Why are we leaving again, when we can just stay up here?" Brithwynn asked, trying to obfuscate the annoyance and frustration she felt. "And why in the middle of the night, on such a dreary night as this?"

"You saw those two men dressed as merchants, the ones who came in just after the rains started hitting in waves?" Valgarðr whispered.

"Yes. What about them?"

"Did you notice anything familiar about them?"

"N-no." Should she have?

"They were dressed as merchants, but they carried themselves like soldiers. And where are their trade goods? Even as merchants they're dressed too well for this establishment, though I suppose it's possible that the storm made them desperate. But merchants always have something to trade, and they don't get wealthy by abandoning it every time there's a little rain."

"You mean –"

"They might be looking for someone else, but we can't risk it. Will you come now?"

"Yes," Brithwynn said, her annoyance forgotten. Or at least redirected.

* * *

The boxlike carriage Valgarðr had borrowed would have served well as a camera obscura and had all the comforts of an oxcart, but it was still better than the roads Valgarðr took them on, deep into the mountains of Macedonia. Their horses spent days, it seemed, pulling the carriage up one narrow, winding goat track, only to spend days working their careful way down the other side.

Valgarðr had bought them flatbread, goat cheese, and olives at the last little town they saw, but Brithwynn and two of the four ladies she had with her found they had little appetite. Only Verina and Juliana were able to stomach their ever-shifting ride in the enclosed carriage.

Brithwynn hated them for it, though she tried not to.

Six days into the mountains, they finally arrived at the small estate that had been in the Maliasenos family since the Empire was ruled from Rome. But the family had absented themselves, and Verina led the ladies into the servants' quarters to sleep and change into peasant garb before continuing on their journey.

Down will be a lot easier, Brithwynn told herself the next morning, as the sun crested over fog-covered mountain peaks. It felt good to be out of that cramped, smelly carriage, even if it meant walking the rough roads in antique leather sandals that felt a little too big.

A few hours later, and Brithwynn wasn't so sure. There was a lot of *up* involved in going down, and her feet felt like they had been rubbed raw by the sand and pebbles that had worked their way into her thick woolen socks.

She rinsed her feet in a small stream they found when they stopped for lunch, but the wayhouse they found that night was the most beautiful thing she'd ever seen.

They had four more days on foot before they would reach Nicopolis and whatever awaited them there.

* * *

"I feel like a scared rabbit, jumping at shadows!" Brithwynn complained quietly to Verina as the older woman brushed out her hair. They had finally made it to Nicopolis, but Valgarðr had kept them mewed up in a small chamber in a rat-infested wayhouse long enough for her feet to heal from their blisters and all but two of her ladies to rejoin them.

Ismenia and her party had actually beaten them to Nicopolis, having had a much more direct route. Their reunion had been a tearful event that put Valgarðr on guard against curious fellow travelers, as the older ladies met with tearful hugs and the younger ones – Thekla and Viviana especially – with near-hysterical shrieks of laughter and tears. The youngest girls barely let go of each other for more than a day as they shared whispered stories of their tribulations and compared road blisters.

Ismenia had smiled indulgently and, with help from Verina and some of the older ladies, gathered an assortment of treats to help the girls overcome their ordeal. The next time he sent one of the Varangians out to get supplies, Valgarðr gave him a few extra coins to get a special treat. Eogan added a basket of dates that earned him the gratitude of all the ladies.

Now Valgarðr and his men sought a safe way for them to cross the broad Danube. Plenty of ferries plied a busy trade between the north and south sides of the river, but Valgarðr sought one who wouldn't ask too many questions or talk too readily if imperial soldiers came around asking questions.

There weren't too many men like that.

"Has there been anyone looking for me since that possible one back in Hadrianopolis?" Though Brithwynn had been cold with fear when they made their escape, it now seemed like nothing more than a distant memory or an absurd nightmare. Their rough passage through the mountains of Macedonia seemed much more real to her than a single encounter with two men who had probably been nothing more than a pair of rich merchants.

"You shouldn't worry about those who come against you openly or with covers as obvious as theirs," Verina said as she began to twist Brithwynn's hair up into a simple chignon. "The one who sends men openly can be avoided. Worry about the ones who come secretly in the night, because their lord will have you killed before you know he wills your death."

"Then how can I ever be safe?" Brithwynn cried, forgetting to hold still as she whipped around to face Verina. "And where? Does Valgarðr intend to just keep me moving until my enemies kill each other off or one of them finds me?"

"You are a porphyrogénita; you will never be safe." Verina told her, trying to make her words hold all the compassion she felt for the young woman who was like a daughter to her. "But God and your father have given you an able servant in Valgarðr, and he will keep you as safe as anyone can."

"I should be grateful, Hypatissa Verina, shouldn't I?" She smiled tightly as she looked up at the older woman who'd always been there for her.

"Even the best of us is only human, my dear," Verina said. "God will understand if you cannot feel gratitude right now, but I have something that might help."

Verina handed Brithwynn the long needle she'd been using to sew her chignon firmly in place and stepped over to the corner where their bags waited for the next hurried escape. In moments, she had pulled a folded piece of papyrus out of a bag and took it over to Brithwynn.

Brithwynn unfolded the papyrus, catching her breath when she recognized Niphon's handwriting. It was a letter from Papa.

Unto the most noble and pure princess, Sebastokratissa Brithwynn of the house of Komnenos doth Alexios, Augoustos of the Basileia tôn Rhōmaiōn and Protector of the Most Holy Church send his most loving paternal greetings on this, the twelfth day of Augostos, in the 6621st year since Creation.

If you are reading this missive, my dearest daughter, I am dead. My own court physicians, the best in the land, are either incapable of curing me or have joined the plot to assassinate me. I pray that their new master receives from them the same laudable service they have given me.

I trust you have left the palace and the Eternal City by the time you read this far. If you did not, if you forced Verina to give you this letter before you would leave the palace, leave now. Do not even wait to finish reading it.

I die from the same vile poison that killed my uncle Isaak before the usurper Romanus IV took the throne. The vipers that fill this palace will mark you for death the moment they decide that you stand between them and the Throne of Solomon, even though most of them are family. It is the malady of the throne, as you well know. Your only safety lies in distance and caution.

Trust no one, save only the Varangian Guard I have placed around you. Trust even them only so long as you are the most powerful member of the Family with access to them. Even their loyalty can be bought, as you have seen in our history. Other than them, only my scribe Niphon and your closest ladies can be trusted, and only so long as they are untainted by other powers.

Your men will take you to the little kingdom of Trimaria, where you will be able to rebuild your forces. Do not argue! I know it is one of the more distant kingdoms in the Empire, far from the Capital and the centers of power, but your mother's family is powerful there and the kingdom is fiercely loyal to them and to Us. You will be safe and will perhaps be able to orchestrate your return to power from there. Or you can choose to rule that one small kingdom and leave the rest of the Empire to eat itself without you.

Use barbarian mercenaries, not any of the Empire's soldiers, whose leaders are too easily bought by palace intriguers. Barbarian loyalties are far more direct and dependable: they are yours as long as you have the gold to pay them and haven't been outbid by someone else they respect. You're safest with ones who have fought for me in one of our previous wars, especially the northern Varangians. Baldar Langstridr Hertogi is the best of them by far, and could easily serve as your right hand if you let him.

My dear child, you are the only one I trust, the only one here who knew your position was strongest while I was alive. You are my chosen Heir, whether you choose Trimaria or the entire Empire.

May God the all-powerful and ever-loving go with you and bless you in all things. I pray that you listen well to these words of warning from an old man who loves you with all the love a father may have for his children, and that you live a long and prosperous life in the light of our Lord's grace before I meet you again in the Paradise of His favor. Pray for me, my beloved daughter.

Alexios Komnenos

Brithwynn surreptitiously wiped her eyes. It didn't really matter if anyone here saw her tears, but too many years in the Blachernai Palace had taught her to be careful and discrete.

So Papa was sending her to her mother's lands, a kingdom so far from Constantinopolis that its people were barely civilized. She had never been there, had never even been outside the Eternal City before this journey. But he had sent her away to protect her and give her the footing to win back the rest of the Empire, and she would use his gift well.

She gestured slightly, and Ariadne hurried to her side. A word, and the kyriatate slipped away to get Niphon.

She had a letter to send.

2

The Winter King

Cold winds from Útgarðr whipped across Lake Lagoda and cut through Ásgarðr, beating ice and snow into the cracks between the logs of the longhouse and keeping the villagers indoors unless necessity forced them outside. The early winter storm made it even more remarkable that a messenger from the great southern empire had reached Ásgarðr, even if he was one of the Rús whose fathers had settled along one of the southern rivers that carried trade goods to and from that great empire. Southern living made the blood soft and thin.

"The Mikligarðr emperor has called for your aid again?" Ása asked, looking with distaste at the papyrus sheet Baldar held.

"No, my hertogakona," Baldar said, looking again at the strange letters the Byzantines used for their messages and which he had learned with difficulty. Runes were so much simpler, though he wondered if they could suffice for the convoluted uses the Byzantines would put them to. Like now.

"Emperor Alexios has died, and told his daughter it was poison," he told Ása. "She requests my aid and offers her hand in marriage to me or any of mine if I will come quickly with a large enough army to defend her kingdom and help her recover the rest of the empire."

"Her hand?" Ása asked, arching her fine brow. "Isn't their Church rather strict about marriage? That might be a problem."

"I could bring our eldest and let him have this... honor," Baldar replied. "Dane's young and strong, she'd marry him in a moment. He could become King of Trimaria, even Emperor of Bysantinsk if the gods are willing."

"And have him die with a knife in the back or by poison like Alexios, so he can never reach Valhalla?" Ása straightened, crossing her arms firmly across her bosom. "You at least would stand a chance in that snake-pit, and have long since earned your place beside the gods. Pick that plum if it's in reach."

* * *

It was an auspicious day for such a gathering, and the turnout was better than Baldar could have hoped for this late in the season. All his own people were there, many having already heard that spring would bring with it the opportunity for wealth and adventure. But many of his oldest and closest allies had also braved the early storms to visit with him over the Jōl fires.

His allies and bondspeople crowded his hall, filling it to the rafters with laughter and song as the fire burned high on his great hearth. Small children and dogs scurried amid the trunk-like legs of the heroes who towered over them or begged food from friendly hands. Girls and young women brought mead and meat to all who filled his hall, but all watched as his beautiful Ása took the Horn of Heroes around to all who had earned word-fame. Though Ása spoke longest with those old heroes she had known since she was a shieldmaiden fighting along-side him, before he had gained the word-fame that now made jarls and hertogis his brothers, she welcomed each of his companions in turn, from old Ragnarr Harðraada to young Ketilgerðr Shieldborn, who had seen her first battles the previous summer.

Behind him, Ljudmilla, Svana, and many of Ása's ladies and guests sat near the wall that separated his sleeping chamber from the rest of the hall, chatting amid baskets of the community's shaggy wool that would be spun and woven into new clothing by Ostara.

Blind Snorri Sigvatr sat close to the fire, where his old limbs were far removed from Útgarðr's chill. Even now, a cluster of Baldar's younger folk listened with bated breath as he told them a story of their people.

It felt like only yesterday when Baldar would have been seated among them in his father's hall back in Vinka across the sea, before his father had blessed him and given him what little he had for a third son, sending him out into the world to make his own way in it.

That way had eventually brought him here, to this little piece of heaven. It had brought him new brothers, ones he would fight with and feast beside from now until Valhalla.

Udvarhelyi and Forgal sat with their shieldbrother Bytor, whose arrival from his lands of Veðrafjorðr in far-off Írlend had already resulted in much ves heilling. Several of the Celtic natives had joined his crew and now drank beside Baldar's men or competed with them at games of skill or daring.

Erika Bjornsdottir, wearing the thick white pelt from the bear she killed as a girl in Grœnlend, sat tall amid the many islanders who followed her. The arrival of this living legend had awed many of Baldar's own men and shieldmaidens, but only Dagný, Magwyn, and Gyða had yet overcome their awe enough to speak with her.

He hoped Erika wasn't telling them too many stories about the youth he'd been.

Þórstenn Wronghand and Haukr Kveldulfsson grappled near the far end of the hearth, surrounded by a crowd of men and shieldmaidens who cheered on their favorite in the perennial sport. From what he could tell, it would be a close and hard-fought contest again.

Þórarinn Brondolfsson and his sister's husband Eiríkr Bludwulf stood quietly watching the grapplers. Though the young Dane was as dark as Þórarinn was fair, they seemed more alike than many real brothers. The quiet way they watched the grapplers told Baldar they were more interested in their tactics than in which of the two men would eventually win. Neither man would grapple amongst their friends for sport, though both had earned word-fame for carrying death to their enemies in empty hands.

Eiríkr had acquitted himself well since becoming one of his men, and the farm Baldar had given them on their marriage to Ástríðr was close enough that Ása hadn't lost one of her best needlewomen. Their eldest son was already one of the taller youths listening to Blind Snorri.

The youngest of the Brondolflingas men, young Þórunn's Gunnvaldr, sat with his bride instead of his new brothers, while Ástríðr and Sólveig chatted beside her and pretended to ignore him. Baldar couldn't blame the boy. He still enjoyed nuzzling with Ása.

Ketilgerðr Shieldborn sat with her mother, the hertogakona the skalds immortalized as a Valkyrie among warriors. Neither marriage nor motherhood had weakened her ax, not when she fought beside her Arnfastr as closely as Freyja beside her brother Freyr. Now their eldest was already gaining word-fame on the battlefield beside them, likely to outdo even her own mother.

Baldar grinned with fierce pride. His people were strong, with alliances forged in the heat of battle to withstand anything short of Ragnorak. As their young grew into adulthood, the strength of their people would only grow. They'd come a long way since Vinka and the few possessions he'd been able to carry with him when he left.

The gathered crowd grew slowly quieter, as the village girls finished bringing food and drink to all and sat down with their families or friends to eat their share. Ása finished sharing out the Horn of Heroes and returned to sit beside him.

"Ves heill!" she said cheerily, handing him the Horn.

"Ves heill!" he replied, quaffing it and returning the Horn so she could have her portion.

* * *

"Companions!" Baldar said, rising to his feet. "Brothers and sisters in arms, friends from far and near! Welcome!"

"Ves heill!" many shouted back, while others shouted "skól!"

"Àsgarðr!" or the names their own people had chosen for themselves. The joyous cacophony rose to the rafters.

"It has been a good year!" he said. "From Grœnlend to Mikligarðr and beyond, our travels have brought us much wealth and word-fame!"

Again they shouted, pounding on tables and stamping on the floor when voices alone proved insufficient.

"When our beautiful sun, beloved of the gods, returns in all her strength, more word-fame will find us! For the dróttning of Mikligarðr in Bysantinsk has summoned us to her lands! There we shall fight her enemies and win much wealth and word-fame to enrich our people!"

"Àsgarðr!" his people shouted, this time joined by many of their allies.

"Who will go with me?" he asked, barely able to hear himself over the noise of his fellow warriors. "Which of you will go with me to the lands of Bysantinsk, that our names might be sung by the skalds of Valhalla?"

Either Þór had just dropped Mjöllnir, or his people were making a thunder that could wake the dead.

Erika was the first to stand. The noise ended abruptly, as everyone waited with bated breath to hear what she would say.

"I will go," she said, sitting down.

"We all go!" one of the larger men seated near her announced, standing and spreading his arms wide to take in the entire Grœnlend contingent. "All the Bjornsfolk."

"My people will be your strong right hand!" Udvarhelvi announced.

"And mine your left!" Forgal declared.

"No!" Þórstenn shouted. "*Mine* is his left! You be his other right!"

"This hand or that," Rædwulf grinned fiercely, "I'll harvest more gold for us than either of you!"

"When have you ever?" Hrothgar asked. "The golden fame you harvest has never equaled mine, nor will it come the spring!"

"Care to wager on that boast?" Rædwulf leered.

"When your harvest equals half of mine," Hrothgar grinned, "I'll give you the other half."

"You boys together haven't harvested half what I have," Annot boasted, hardly exaggerating. "I'll give you a chance to catch up this time, though I doubt you can."

"I might just have you beat!" Svipdag bragged, as others tried to claim a greater harvest than the old shieldwoman.

Háftan Ironoak waited until the noise and boasting had died down. "I'll go, with my men," he said quietly. "I've always wanted to visit Miklegarðr and see all those stone buildings they have there. That big old church especially. From what I hear, it's got everything but some runes that say 'Háftan was here.'"

"You and your runes!" someone laughed. "How long do you expect them to stay up in a *church*?"

"Till Ragnorak," Háftan replied. "If that church's really made of stone."

Þórarinn Brondolfsson had been conferring with his father and sister's husband. "The Brondolflingas are with you," he said, rising as Háftan sat.

"*All* the Brondolflingas!" Àstriðr shot back, after exchanging looks with Sólveig and Þórunn.

"Àsgarðr is your home," Eiríkr replied, groaning good-naturedly. "You should stay and tend the farm."

"You think we'd let you have all the fun?" Sólveig asked, laughing. "Have you forgotten where you met us?"

"Come, then," Eiríkr laughed. "You will anyway!"

"Good," Àsa said quietly, leaning toward him. "Àstriðr has learned to decipher their runes now too, not just ours. She reads them faster than you now and can even write them."

Baldar glanced over at her and nodded. A scribe he could trust in that snakepit could be invaluable.

"I go where my brothers go!" young Gunnvaldr declared, standing up abruptly as he noticed that Þórarinn and Eiríkr had joined the great war-party.

"Not always!" Bytor boomed.

Gunnvaldr reddened slightly as he realized that everyone could see he was nearly surrounded by women, far from his two new brothers and most of the other warriors of repute.

"Would you, if you could sit with these ladies?" Gunnvaldr retorted, recovering quickly with an almost-skaldic wit. "They smell better than you!"

"They look better, too!" Þórstenn laughed.

"Weak works are short praise," Bytor rumbled, rising to his feet and lifting his horn cup toward the rafters. His resounding skaldic voice filled the hall. "But beauty's lack is little loss for men of war. Once more, great heroes of the North, for Baldar and renown fight now in glorious distant fields. Led as by Tyr, they crush with ax and sword the limbs of those who rise against the dróttning of Bysantinsk, till none remain to offer battle's bloody work." He drained the cup, letting it drop to the table below. "And to this host I bring my own small einherjar, enough to take the gates of Mikligarðr itself."

"Thank you, brother," Baldar said in the silence that followed, as the rest of the hall realized the full impact of Bytor's grand words.

The silence didn't last more than a moment. When it ended, the hall erupted as hero after hero announced that he – or she – would also answer Brithwynn's call. The Sea Wolves would be there, as would the Black Swords and the Ice Bears. The Bloody Swords and Tyrni followed before Bjarni of the Ice Bears could sit, followed by the Hakonarlingas and the Sturlingas. Yngvilðr swore to bring the warriors of the Geirrlingas. House Greywulf would bring six tylpts of men and ships for as many more. Eydís Hugleikrsdóttir would bring her men and shieldmaidens, and Olgar Bjornkló would be there with his own small following. Ulfgestr said he could bring two ships' worth of warriors. Arnfastr added that the Wulflingas would be there with a dozen ships, and Forgal declared that his people would best them with twice tylpt. Bjorn Osgkarsen had nearly a tylpt of ships in various stages of completion and would build more over the winter for any who needed them. He could fill six with his men and shieldmaidens.

Tyr had blessed him with more warriors than he had dreamed would follow him to Bysantinsk.

And yet –

This was too many. Too many by far, with no sign that it would stop until each hero in the hall had declared that he would go.

Baldar's blood ran cold as he recognized the Trickster's handiwork. Too many of his friends and allies had answered the call.

Baldar glanced over at Àsa. Had she realized yet that his call to arms had destroyed Àsgarðr? How long before their enemies discovered that he'd left it undermanned and ill-guarded?

From the tightness around her mouth, she realized it. Knowing her, she would let him take all Àsgarðr's fighting force and allies, determined to protect their land with old men, children, and those women who had hung up their shields for a mother's distaff.

And she would succeed. Somehow.

But he would not leave her with such a meager fighting force.

"Brothers! Sisters!" he cried. "I know well your taste for battle and long journeys, for I have been beside you when you sought them! But I ask a greater challenge of you now. Which of you will remain here, to guard our home for our return? Which of you will stay to keep our families secure, that Àsgarðr may remain here until our last warriors are called to Valhalla?"

"You have a lot of enemies around here, brother!" Þórstenn declared. "Wends, Letts, Ástis, a couple Finnish chieftains…"

"Finnr and Úgli, if you can call them 'chieftains'!" Rædwulf shouted, to uproarious laughter.

"I'd like to finish off old Finnr!" Vikarr declared, fingering the ax he was never without.

"I bet you would!" Hafgrimr laughed, as the hall erupted into uproarious guffaws. Several men seated between the two moved quickly to get out of the way in case a fight erupted.

"You can play with him first, brother," Vikarr quipped, laughing as he raised his horn to his companion. "My ax'll be happy with whatever's left."

The hall reverberated with laughter as the two old warriors decided to drink instead of fight. Brawling could wait till later.

"My sons and I will stay!" Olgar Bjornkló declared as the laughter died down. His two young sons, Ragnar and Vakri, tried valiantly to hide their disappointment at the prospect of staying home in Àsgarðr when all the world seemed to be accompanying Baldar, but their father's announcement was not the last.

"I have become an old man," old Ragnarr Harðraada said, using his walking stick to stand. "My arms have become palsied, and my legs have become too weak to carry me far beyond our shores," he added. "But I will fight and die for Àsa, if she ever needs me."

"You lie," Baldar said, his voice dark and cold. "You still have many good years left to you." He smiled at their joke, and his tone changed completely. "And I'm glad you've chosen to spend them here with Àsa."

"Brother!" Brondolf Far-Traveled declared, standing up. "We have gone on many journeys together and seen much of the world. We have sailed the Frozen Sea to the Gunnbjorn Skerries and journeyed to the fabled markets of Serklend. But this time, I stay here. I have become too old for such a young man's journey. This time, I offer my ax to Àsa Hertogakona. My children – all but the youngest and her man – shall go with you to Trimaria of Bysantinsk. You shall have my children, and I shall have yours."

"May we both benefit from this exchange, brother," Baldar said, taking the older man's offered arm in his and enfolding him in a hug.

"I will stay here," Háftan said as he looked up from the table where his knife traced delicate runes across the surface.

"I thought you wanted to see all their stone buildings?" Ulfgestr asked.

"I still do," Háftan said. "But that can wait a couple years, till young Sten's ready to see the world. That big old church isn't going away any-time soon."

"Not if it's made of stone, anyway," Valbranðr laughed.

"You can be Baldar's left hand this time," Þórstenn told Forgal. "I'll stay here and be Àsa's left."

"And a good left hand it is," Baldar grinned at him. "Not like your right."

The bantering continued well into the night, as the fire crackled and the people who meant the most to him put away a significant quantity of the mead he'd stored up for the winter. Ædrick Hamarskald stood at one point to sing from the *Saga of Sigurðr*, and Corwyn of Veðrafjorðr sang a song that brought the company to tears.

It was a good Jōl.

He and Àsa both had warriors enough for the need, and they would not be the last. More of his friends and allies would come by spring, as word spread slowly in the depths of winter and opened men's hearts to the call of adventure.

He might need a few more ships.

* * *

"Listen well, for this may be the last advice I give you!" Baldar leaned back against the great ash tree that reigned over the promontory high above Àsgarðr and Lake Ladoga. It offered some protection against the brisk spring winds, but it would be at least a month before the ice roads melted and Baldar was glad that Eden had left her firstborn in the hall with Àsa. She and Àsa the Younger – his little Àsaka - sat close at his feet, while the boys stood behind them, automatically standing guard near the edge of the promontory.

Their children were strong saplings, ones that belonged here in this harsh northern land, where his people were free. He could only thank Àsa and the gods for that, and that he had this land of Àsgarðr to leave them.

"First and last," Baldar told them, "I ask that you always remember to take care of your mother and the holdings. If she marries another, judge him by how he treats her when you don't seem to be looking." He paused, eyeing each of their children in turn. "*Always* be looking."

"You don't expect to ever return," Eden said, surprised but calm. "Not this time."

The others glanced at her in shock, then looked to him for an answer.

"No, my children," Baldar replied. "This is more than just some summer journey. Whether I marry this girl or just fight her battles, I'll be needed in Trimaria till the gods summon me home."

"Then why go?" Dane asked. "When you have all this already?" His gesture encompassed all of Àsgarðr, from the massive convocation of dragon ships on their high sledges gathered on the edge of Lake Ladoga to the bustling village and the outer meadows, where herdsmen were already taking herds out to fatten on the early spring grasses.

"*This* is why," Baldar replied. "Àsgarðr is greater than my father's lands of Vinka, but it's not big enough for all of you. Dane stands to inherit it, as my eldest brother inherited Vinka. The three ships I'm leaving you won't row themselves, Sten, and it's only our friendships and alliances that will fill them. *You* must fill them, with the fame I've brought us and your own. And my girls? Eden married well, but only because my word-fame and her mother's beauty made her a desirable catch. We still need to find a good husband for little Àsaka," he said, smiling at his younger daughter and the reindeer fawn she held. It had grown well as she nursed it through the winter.

He hoped that fawn was an omen of his children's future.

"Not-so-little Àsaka," he corrected himself. "He must be a great man like Eden's Þórðr, who will take good care of her. That kind of a husband only comes with powerful alliances."

"Then stay here and make them!" Sten argued. "What can you do in Bysantinsk?"

"In Bysantinsk, nothing," Baldar replied. "But my old friend Alric of Gardariki has been considering her for his eldest. I can finalize arrangements for her marriage on my way south, and my journey to Bysantinsk will seal the deal. Alric will want to tighten his relations to the king of Trimaria, even more than he wants to tighten them with the lord of Àsgarðr."

"Do we *want* that kind of friendship?" Dane asked, his tone firmly negative.

"Whether we want it or not is shapes in the fog," Baldar replied, remembering when he had been naïve enough for such questions. "It is the way of the world, and we must work within it if we are to succeed in it. You boys must understand that when the time comes to choose your own brides."

"And with your alliances of all kinds," Baldar added. "Shield-sibs will you grow rich in, both among these friends of mine," Baldar gestured expansively out at the valley below, where his own shieldbrothers were gathering for their journey south, "and among new friends you meet, but never forget that some will play you false while others are as true as the sibs you see beside you."

"You four must *always* be true to one another, even if the Nornir will that you are the only ones you can count on. Be worthy of each other's loyalty, and that of those other shield-sibs you gain."

The girls had reached out their hands to each other as he spoke, a gesture that moved him now more than it usually did. He must be getting soft. They looked up at their brothers, who nodded manfully at each other before smiling back at the girls.

"Anyone would have to be a fool to attack any of us!" Sten declared.

"True," Dane replied. "But there are fools enough here in Midgarðr."

"Well said, the both of you," Baldar said. "And that is why you must never seek to make an enemy. But if *he* should be so foolish as to seek *you*, then send him on to the Cold Lady without warning and without compunction. Leave no enemy behind, for they will rise up and spring for your throat. Never wound slightly, for it is never enough."

All the children nodded unconsciously as he said these familiar words, for he and Àsa had drummed the danger of a 'conquered' foe into them since they were too young for their first daggers. It had served to keep them alive and well-blooded in their first battles.

But they could all work on the next of Odin's proverbs. He had been no different at their age, like most young men and maidens. They would learn, hopefully without too much bloodshed.

"Trust not in sweet words, but observe what the stranger does and treat him accordingly. Praise no day till it has ended, nor sword till swung in battle. Neither trust a maiden till she's bedded –"

"Faðir!" Eden exclaimed.

"No, nor a man either," Baldar continued, putting up a hand to quiet her objections. "Not till he's gotten what he wants and still treats you well when the guests are gone home."

The children exchanged glances, as Sten and Dane stiffened. They had helped to outcast a niðingr two winters ago who had acted as if his woman and children were his battle-prizes.

"Men's true selves are only seen when they think themselves safe and secure. So you must watch them, *especially* at such times. Know yourself and your foe. If he be stronger than you, pacify him with sweet words until you are stronger –"

"But that's cowardice!" Sten objected.

"No, that's wisdom. Cowardice is avoiding the fight because you're afraid. Strategy is delaying your battle till you can fight it on your chosen battlefield. Wisdom will tell you which is which."

* * *

Baldar stayed on the promontory long after he'd shared the last bit of wisdom he could think of and talked with his four treasures until there was nothing more to say. He stayed till each of them had to leave, till even the beautiful sun dipped low on the horizon and the night winds rose to cut, knifelike, through his furs and woolen clothes.

"You seek your home, my lady," Baldar whispered to the blushing sun, "and I'll seek mine. Keep those who live there safe while I'm away."

The sun was gathering in the last rays of evening by the time Baldar passed the last of his people's homes and all the gardens and animal pens that surrounded them. He stopped to speak with several of them, though his thoughts were on Ása the entire time. Had he done enough to help her and the children through his absence?

He opened the great door of the house he and Ása had built together when they first came to this little piece of heaven, half expecting the place to be crowded with his people and their allies.

It wasn't. Ása stood alone in front of the hearth, looking every bit the young shieldmaiden she'd been when he first met her. A couple tapers hanging from the rafters lit her golden face and kept her from being a darkened silhouette against the small cookfire that burned in the hearth.

Ása stepped toward him for a quick kiss, then turned back toward the hearth and the simple supper that waited next to the fire.

"We have the place to ourselves tonight," she said. "I made –"

"That's not what I want, my heart-queen," Baldar murmured, breathless. "Come back here."

"You too," she said, coming into his arms.

* * *

Baldar left the house later than he'd planned the next morning. He walked hand in hand with Ása till they were almost to the frozen lake and the dozens of ships that awaited him there, then stopped and wrapped her in his arms one last time.

"I'll see you again," he said, breathing in the scent of her. "In Fensalir, if not before."

"Oh, you'll come visit me once in a while," she replied as she kissed him and pushed him gently away, "when you want a break from all the drinking and fighting in Valhalla. How is that any different from what we have here?"

3

Amazonia

The horses Valgarðr purchased for them as they entered Ansteoria's horse-lords country were a godsend, though they gave her blisters in places she couldn't imagine. Brithwynn couldn't have faced another day on foot, nor one enclosed in another camera obscura masquerading as a form of transportation. She insisted that they stay on horseback till they came to the swamps at the mouth of the Dniester and had to leave them behind to make the crossing into Glenabenia in the local flat-bottomed boats.

And the first thing she did when they reached solid ground on the other side was make Valgarðr find replacement mounts.

Though most of her ladies had no more experience riding than Brithwynn did, Verina was the only one still uncomfortable on horseback by the time they were a week into Ansteoria. Even Niphon and the maids who'd chosen to remain with them slowly became skilled riders, while Viviana and Thekla became true amazons on horseback. The horses' greater speed made grasslands and forests alike slip away underfoot faster than Brithwynn could have believed, much faster than the old carriage they had ridden in to Maliasenos lands.

The countryside they rode through was bright with the red and gold leaves of autumn, though the chill in the air bespoke colder weather soon to come. Riding through the open countryside in a simple woolen gown and a pair of soft linen breeches of the type worn for centuries by the Empire's barbarian cavalry turned the journey into an adventure instead of a series of tribulations. Even Valgarðr's choice of wayhouses improved, unless she was just getting accustomed to them.

For the first time in her life, Brithwynn truly felt free.

A part of her hoped this journey would never end, though her logical side knew it must. No palace could ever offer the freedom of a horse, but she couldn't stay on a horse forever.

"Your father would be proud to see you like this, Princess," Valgarðr said as he rode up on her left, breaking her reverie.

"He would?" Brithwynn asked, surprised that Valgarðr could think that the sight of her in this disheveled state would make her father proud. She smelled like horse, and Verina had given up on keeping even a simple bun in place. As long as they were on horseback, Brithwynn and her ladies wore barbarian braids.

"Truly," he replied. "Your mother was a princess when he met her, but she was a wild Trimarian princess. Almost a barbarian, the way they ride and fight in a way that no Byzantine noble would, not even the men. He was amazed, called her an Amazon. I think that's when he decided to marry her."

Brithwynn had never heard any of this. Her father had barely ever talked about her mother since she died in childbirth soon after Isaak was born. When he, or anyone else in the palace, had mentioned her at all, it was only as Empress Anastasiya, the princess from an outer principality who had become Augousta of all Rhōmania. Only her stepmother Maria had dared to say anything remotely derogatory about her, and that only once she had a couple imperial sons to benefit from her attempts to denigrate a previous empress.

Even she hadn't exactly *said* that Anastasiya had been a wild barbarian, just that she had been somewhat lacking in those particular social graces that made a noblewoman fit to be the empress.

Brithwynn didn't care. She'd scarcely been ten when she realized that her stepmother would do anything to put one of her own sons on the

Throne of Solomon. From that point on, anything the Empress Maria said or did was highly suspect, as were her opinions on all subjects.

It was then that she began to adore the mother she barely remembered.

"You knew my mother back then?" she asked.

"Not really. I was just a young warrior at the time, in the einherjar – that's a war band, like a tagma – of my lord, Önund. He had taken service with your father when a tribe of Mongols attacked the northeastern borders of the Empire. Trimaria was on the border back then, and your grandfather sent three armies. Your mother led one."

"She *led* one?" Brithwynn asked, amazed.

"From the front," Valgarðr replied. "Like a real warlord. That's the way we northern barbarians fight."

"Tell me about her," Brithwynn commanded.

"What... what would you like to know, Princess?" Valgarðr asked.

Something about his tone made Brithwynn turn and look at the old Varangian.

He was blushing.

"You loved her!" she exclaimed.

If anything, that made him blush harder. The fiery redness spread across his face and down past his beard to disappear under his tunic and burnished lamellar cuirass.

"No... yes," he stuttered. "Or no. I worshipped her as a goddess, the way every young man loves a woman he knows he can never aspire to even touch."

"Because she was a princess?"

"That, and more, Princess. She had the bearing of an ancient hero of my people, on the battlefield and off. When she entered a room, everyone turned to her as if they knew she was truly the one in command. Even your father did, and he was already a greater commander than Ióannés at that age. Skalds could sing of her exploits, and many did. And when she rode a horse or strode through camp..."

"Yes?"

"With her red hair flowing and her fur-lined coat, the princess looked like one of the ancient go- er, saints of my people."

"I wish I could see her," Brithwynn said, half-aloud.

"You can, Princess," Valgarðr replied, as his blush once more advanced toward his neckline. "Out here on horseback, you look like her. You're even gaining her bearing. Only your hair and clothes are different."

"Thank you," Brithwynn said. It didn't feel like the right thing to say, but she didn't know what was.

* * *

"Won't we be in danger if they learn who I am?" Brithwynn asked, looking with trepidation at the small hill-town before them. It bore the noble name of Glenopolis, but not long ago she would have overlooked it entirely, sure that no noble habitation could be found within its wooden walls. Now the certainty that one would meant it was surely a danger to be avoided.

Almost as much a danger as the grey cloud that loomed from horizon to horizon behind them, blown up from the shores of the Black Sea. Even now, the wind was starting to pick up and fat droplets impacted around them. Lightning forked across the sky in the darkest part of the cloud, promising worse to come.

"No, Princess," Valgarðr replied. "Glenabenia and the other kingdoms out here might be part of the Empire, but in their souls they're barbarian Rús. And we don't give up one of our own to an outsider, no matter what force is applied."

He grinned fiercely, his teeth showing. "We actually *like* it when people try to use force on us. The odds tend to not be in their favor."

"But Princess," he added, just as she was about to nudge her horse forward. "Here you must give them the means to pretend they don't know who you are. You should be... Eiríni, returning home to Trimaria after visiting family in Ansteoria. That will tell them everything they need to know and nothing they don't want to know, yet."

At her quizzical look, he added, "Peace, claiming family in Ansteoria and Trimaria."

"I know what the name means!" Brithwynn exclaimed. "But what significance do those two kingdoms have, other than that you named our real destination?"

"I forget how little you know about the outer kingdoms of the Empire," Valgarðr said, nudging his horse forward. "For now, you just need to know that those two kingdoms were at war with each other for generations, before they joined the Empire. And Glenabenia was often the site of those battles. The people you meet here will read the message there."

"Eiríni," Brithwynn said, nudging her horse into a canter. "It's a good name!"

* * *

Valgarðr took the lead as they entered the quiet town, easily gaining admittance from the guards at the outer gate. As they rode up the hill toward the fortified palace at its crest, Brithwynn couldn't help noticing that nearly every house bristled with bows or axes trained on them.

A sudden chill shook her, one that had nothing to do with the rains that had finally caught up with them in force. Glenopolis had opened so readily to them because it would be their deaths.

But there was nowhere else to go, and the storm would be their deaths just as surely if they stayed out in it.

Brithwynn had to take comfort in Valgarðr's apparent lack of concern. He had gotten them this far, when the outlook had been far more grim.

He would know a trap when he rode into it, even when it was set on them by his own people.

Wouldn't he?

The narrow street turned sharply again before opening up into a small plaza, where a simple fountain was almost hidden by sheets of rain. On the other side of the fountain, a sturdy fortified house of simple undressed fieldstone rose above its neighbors.

"Welcome to the palace of Glenopolis!" Valgarðr called out to her before riding forward to the doors that opened to them as he spoke.

* * *

"My lady Eiríni of Trimaria begs shelter for the night," Brithwynn heard Valgarðr announce to the guards posted at the house's small gate, hardly larger than most doors in the Blachernae. "Shelter for herself and fify-two members of her household retinue."

A figure Brithwynn could barely see through the rain ran into the main part of the house and returned minutes later. The guards at the door parted and Valgarðr gestured her forward.

Brithwynn rode into the sheltered gate passage and had to nudge her horse forward when it tried to stop there. Several grooms awaited her in the arcaded porch ahead of her, and she rode forward, conscious that Valgarðr and another Varangian flanked her just a step or two behind.

Two Glenabenian grooms helped her dismount, and Valgarðr turned her to the right, where a set of wide brick steps rose to the entrance to the house itself.

Inside was warmth. Brithwynn had barely crossed the threshold when two young ladies approached and wrapped her in a thick linen towel that reached to her toes, one that had been warmed by the fire for the benefit of the queen or one of their guests. She turned to glance at Valgarðr as the girls drew her forward toward the queen and the U-shaped grouping of tables around a brazier full of red-hot coals that filled the far side of the large room.

He nodded subtly, a smile breaking the somber expression he usually wore. Behind him, many of her ladies had already entered the hall and been wrapped in their own linen towels.

If this was a trap, even Valgarðr couldn't see it.

She stepped forward toward the queen, doing her best to remember from her etiquette lessons how lesser royals were to be approached in their own lands... or anywhere.

Her lessons had been sorely lacking in that regard, for a porphyrogénita never bowed to anyone who was not also purple-born.

She eventually decided to mimic the rustic courtesies she had seen visitors from the northern kingdoms use in her father's court.

Even that was too much. The queen rushed forward, taking her hands in her own.

"My dear! You're chilled to the bone!" she declared, drawing Brithwynn over near the brazier. "Come in and warm yourself up! My ladies have dry clothes if you and yours would like to change. Or you can eat first; we have plenty."

Brithwynn felt overwhelmed by the queen's unexpected generosity and looked to Valgarðr for guidance.

He nodded again, a peaceful smile she had never seen before suffusing his features. It made him look different, younger.

Could this truly be the first time she had ever seen him unconcerned for her safety?

"Thank you, Your Majesty," Brithwynn said, turning back to the queen. "Your hospitality is much appreciated. And I believe we"ll dry off first, then change and join you at your repast."

"It's the least we could do for travelers caught out on the road in this weather," the queen replied. "And 'Ióanna' is sufficient. 'Basilissa Ióanna' if you need to be formal."

"Ióanna, then," Brithwynn replied. "Please, call me Eiríni." A thought suddenly struck her. "But weren't you about to start your dinner?" she added. "I wouldn't want to delay you."

"Oh no," Basilissa Ióanna laughed. "We await my husband and his men. They're out checking the levees, as they do whenever it rains heavily. But they should return soon."

"Levees?" Brithwynn asked.

"I'm sorry," Basilissa Ióanna replied. "They're such a daily part of life here that one tends to forget they don't have levees everywhere. And if you have levees in Trimaria, you probably call them by some other name. Much of our land is low-lying, it would even be swampland if we didn't raise it up and wall it off from the rivers. Those walls are what we call levees. But whenever it rains heavily here or upstream, the rivers swell and the levees are in danger of giving way. So each noble is responsible for maintaining the levees on his lands and patrolling them during times of heavy rain or flooding."

"If we have those, I think we must have some other name for them," Brithwynn replied, trying to recall everything she'd been told about Trimaria. "Or maybe Father just didn't talk about them with me."

"That's not unlikely," Basilissa Ióanna said thoughtfully. "You're young, and such quotidian matters are hardly ones he would speak of to a daughter. Men are often mute about those things they think we need not know. But my sons are old enough to help their father patrol the levees."

Brithwynn realized who the towels must have been prepared for.

"True," she replied, thinking of all the lessons in statecraft her father had imparted to her over the years. He had surely covered everything, even how to maintain the types of infrastructure that must include things like levees.

His rule for such matters belonged under the heading "Delegation." Papa had been a firm believer in the truism that the best way to get a job done was to find the right man for the job and give him enough tax money to do it right. But he had ruled the Empire, a land so vast that even the emperors of old had been forced to delegate much of their power. Out here in the provinces, lesser kings had neither the need nor the ability to delegate to such an extent.

And she must help how she could, even if it was only to ensure he and his men could dry off in warm towels on their return.

"I believe we're dry enough to change clothes," she said, after patting her sleeve as if checking how dry she'd gotten.

"Oh, certainly! My ladies will get you some dry clothes to change into," the queen said, with one final squeeze of Brithwynn's hands. Raising her voice a little and looking over at the cluster of ladies who were helping Brithwynn's people spread their cloaks to dry – mainly by taking over the job and cajoling them toward the warmth of the fire – she continued, "Magdalena, ladies, please take our guests to find some dry clothes. Something nice and warm."

Several of the queen's ladies left the others to finish hanging up the last of the wet things and approached the queen, giving her a quick bob and looking and Brithwynn with expressions evidencing combinations of curiosity and friendliness.

"Thank you, my dear," Ióanna said to the first of her ladies to approach, a slender girl with dark, curly hair. "Eiríni, my dear, this is the Prinkepissa Magdalena, my eldest's wife. She's like a daughter to me, and I hope will be like a sister to you while you're with us."

Brithwynn hoped she wouldn't. One of her earliest memories was of her older half-sister Euphrosyne taking away her first strand of pearls because "babies don't wear pearls." They'd always had an antagonistic, if distant, relationship – one that hadn't been ameliorated by their step-mother or nurses.

"Oh, you are wet!" Magdalena said, gracing Brithwynn with a dazzling smile. "Come with me, and we'll get you and your ladies into something dry and warm."

Without another word, she took Brithwynn's hand and led her off to the back of the hall, followed by Brithwynn's ladies and several of the locals. They proceeded through a couple short passageways and up a flight of stairs before Magdalena threw open a door.

"It's quite a labyrinth in here, I know," she said with a wink and another dazzling smile. "But you'll learn your way around soon enough. This room is where most of the unmarried ladies sleep, where I slept before the wedding. I think I still have some things in here you can use, and I know some of the other ladies do."

The room beyond was simple but well-plastered and large enough to comfortably hold several beds and large chests. Two braziers held a few coals each, just enough to warm the room and stave off the chill that seeped in from the rains that beat against the shutters that covered the room's windows.

It was the nicest bedroom she'd been in since the Blachernae.

"What's your favorite color?" Magdalena asked as she glided across the room, half-dragging Brithwynn along with her. "Your family's colors? We probably have something you'd like."

She reached one of the larger chests and started pulling out gowns. A young girl who followed them draped the gowns across the closest bed for Brithwynn's perusal, while a dark-haired girl went to the other chest between that bed and the one next to it and started pulling out more gowns.

She had been born to the purple, but to say so would be death if the wrong people learned of it.

"Red," Brithwynn said quickly, "and blue."

"You would look lovely in blue," the other girl said.

"Oh, Eiríni," Magdalena said, turning from her own chest of clothes long enough to take Brithwynn's hand in hers and slip her other arm around the other girl's waist. "This is my dear sister Milica. She just married Steph's younger brother, and she has *wonderful* taste in clothes."

Milica blushed delicately as she looked from Magdalena to Brithwynn and smiled.

"Magdalena's too kind," she said. "But I'm glad you got here when you did. And I think I have the perfect dress for you."

She pulled a few more gowns from the chest before removing a bright blue wool gown and holding it up between her and Brithwynn. "Here," she said, handing it to her. "This'll be beautiful on you."

"Oh yes," Magdalena said, looking from Brithwynn to the gown in her hands. "That one looks like it was made for you."

It was beautiful, Brithwynn thought, a blue that matched the skies during their ride through Ansteoria or the color of the Mamora on a clear day. And the wool it was made of was light and smooth, woven into a crisp twill.

"I love it," she said.

"It is yours," Milica replied.

"No," Brithwynn countered. "You can't just give me one of your gowns!"

"I already have." She smiled triumphantly, but without any trace of the sly cruelty Brithwynn had often seen in Euphrosyne's smiles. "Can we get you anything else?"

* * *

A commotion at the gate outside brought the Court to its feet, even before one of the guards opened the door and a large number of fighting men rushed in, their weapons and armor heavily splattered with mud and glistening with raindrops that had gotten through their oiled cloaks.

Brithwynn wanted to run in terror, certain that Ióannés' men had somehow found her.

For them to continue searching this far from Constantinopolis, and in this weather, they must be under orders that left little doubt about her fate.

Valgarðr had made a terrible mistake, one that would surely get her killed, along with all her people. Perhaps even the people of Glenopolis, if they weren't quick enough to hand her over.

Brithwynn managed to sag behind Basilissa Ióanna's matronly bulk, just as the first of the warriors began shedding their oiled cloaks and stomping mud off their boots.

"Don't track that muck in here!" Basilissa Ióanna commanded, striding forward toward the warriors as the hall erupted with cries of "All hail Basilios Iakovos!"

They were safe.

For now.

Probably.

If Basilios Iakovos believed her story.

* * *

"I hope you aren't in too much of a rush to leave us, my dear," Ióanna said to her three days later as they broke their fast over a light meal of the previous day's leftover bread with olives, fragrant cheese, and fish from the local rivers.

"Indeed not!" Basilios Iakovos boomed from the other side of the queen. "We haven't had a breach yet –"

"Thank the Lord!" Basilissa Ióanna breathed, fingering her rosary.

"But many of the roads are underwater, or so close that I wouldn't send you out in this till the flooding starts to go down," he continued.

"How long do you think that will be?" Brithwynn asked. No matter how good it felt to be here with these people, she couldn't ask them to risk themselves for her sake any longer than necessary, especially since they didn't really know who she was or who was after her.

"This time of year, it can rain for days, weeks at a stretch," Basilios Iakovos replied. "And then you have to let the roads dry for a few more days, so you don't end up sinking into it somewhere and laming a good horse. But don't worry, you're more than welcome to stay here as long as you need."

"Longer, if you're not in a rush to get back home," Ióanna added with a heartwarming smile.

"Be warned," Iakovos added, shaking his head and grinning. "I think she's already trying to match you up with one of our nobles, so you never have to leave."

Brithwynn wished she could take them up on the offer.

* * *

A week later, the heavy rains had raised water levels behind all the levees well above normal flood levels. Basilios Iakovos took most of his household guard and all the able-bodied men of Glenopolis out daily to patrol the levees and build up any place where the waters reached too high up the banks, but there were dangers they could only guess at. The roads leading to several of the levees were flooded in places, making them unreachable. And, as Iakovos explained one evening, even where they could patrol the embankments, the roiling dark waters hid dangers lurking beneath. Debris in the floodwaters or even the waters themselves could erode the levees far below the surface, till suddenly a sturdy-looking stretch of levee gave way and released the floodwaters into the land behind it.

Brithwynn was glad she had been allowing Valgarðr to take her men out to help patrol the levees, though she now resolved to have Valgarðr find out what danger signs to look for. If they didn't already know, which was extremely likely.

"Are the rains always this bad?" she asked.

"No, not often," he replied. "This seems to be a bad year for flooding. But we're getting less and less each day, so we can hope it'll end soon."

Brithwynn wanted to ask why they would choose to live in a place that suffered from such terrible flooding, but she didn't know quite how to ask.

Ióanna seemed to see the question on her lips.

"It's beautiful here most of the time," she said, her voice warmed by her great love for her land and its people. "The land is among the most fruitful in the Empire, and it serves us well. Besides, it is home."

"You should know," she added. "Your homeland is the same."

* * *

Basilios Iakovos and his men should have been back by now.

The rain had long since tapered off to an intermittent patter, and both the brazier and oil lamps had needed to be refilled. The sky outside had cleared enough for them to see a colorful sunset where rich royal hues competed with each other for precedence. But now darkness stretched across the sky and covered the earth beneath.

It was a new day, one that filled Brithwynn with foreboding.

At first she'd thought she was just being impatient, but as she looked around the hall Brithwynn realized that grim expectancy suffused the features of nearly everyone there. Even the children had quieted, subconsciously taking their cue from their elders.

It wasn't normal for the men to stay out so long after the rains ended, not when there had been no report of a breach. Nobody knew what had caused the delay, but everyone had fears of what it might portend.

* * *

Well after sunset, after their nurses or mothers took the last of the household's children off to bed, sounds of horsemen outside caused everyone to look around with renewed hope.

But it lasted mere moments. Even through the door, they could tell that the men were not their usual tired but ebullient selves.

Something had gone terribly wrong.

As she exchanged looks with Magdalena, she realized that the other girl knew it as well and was afraid of what it could be. Milica looked even more terrified, as her eyes went huge and round and her face drained of color.

Ióanna was as white as a ghost. The beads of her rosary whirled through her fingers as she prayed.

As she looked around the room, Brithwynn realized that everyone knew what such a late return meant.

Something terrible had happened to keep the men out so long. And while there were many possibilities, the worst was also the most likely.

A levee had broken. At least one person had been killed, or wounded so badly that death was likely.

They just didn't know who.

Brithwynn groped for Milica's hand. It *probably* wasn't one of her men; there were only thirty of them.

But that meant it was probably a Glenabenian. And three of them were very important to the ladies she was starting to think of as family.

The room was silent as everyone waited to see who they had lost. Even the ladies preparing bandages and splints did so without any of the conversation or little noises that usually filled the hall.

When the doors swung open, the place could have been a sepulcher.

"No!" Basilissa Ióanna exclaimed, standing abruptly.

She took one step toward the body being carried in and sank to the floor.

Brithwynn dropped to her knees beside the fallen queen, checking for some sign of life. She felt, rather than saw, Milica join her and start fanning the older woman.

In the back of her mind, Brithwynn realized she was looking for signs that Ióanna had been poisoned. But it was probably something far less Byzantine.

With a growing sense of dread, Brithwynn looked up from the queen's unconscious form, past Magdalena, who appeared frozen in place, to the body being carried into the hall.

It was the elder prince, Stephanos.

The prince's once-perfect body had been beaten and broken by the floodwaters as it had never been in life. It lay draped across the shields of his men, whose faces told of their own great sorrow.

Then the prince's shieldbearers staggered forward to place their lord on the benches several of the ladies had pulled together near the center of the room, and Brithwynn saw the king. He was caked in mud up to his armpits, and his face made her worry that a heart attack was imminent.

Her own men's arrival was anticlimactic. She barely noticed that Brendan and Ragnar were carrying Rafn.

* * *

Prinkeps Ængelos had maneuvered his mother out of Basilios Iakovos' sickroom long enough to speak with the household doctor, but the look in her eyes gave him little hope that she would listen, or even could. Her husband's sudden illness, coming on as it did right after Stephanos' death, was simply too much for her to face.

"Your Majesty, Basilios Iakovos cannot patrol the levees this day." Methodios, the household doctor, repeated with professional calm. "Nor, likely, for another week. He is become too sanguine, and the tragic loss of the elder prince thickened his blood till it became almost too thick to flow through his body and remove excess bile and phlegm. He needs rest and a good bloodletting, with plenty of good red wine to refresh his blood. Else you will lose him, as well."

"By God, the levees must be patrolled!" Ængelos swore, turning to his mother. "Father cannot, but it is our duty to see it done and I *will not* leave the job to some *subordinate*!"

"I cannot lose you too!" Ióanna wailed, her whole body shaking with the tears she tried to stem as she looked up at her younger son, grown into such responsibility long before Fate should have asked it of him. "I cannot! Would you leave us a household of grieving women?"

"You will not lose me, Mother," Ængelos said, trying to soften his voice though the frustration and loss made him want to push through to the outcome he knew was necessary.

The outcome his mother knew was necessary, though she could not face it after so much loss.

He wrapped Ióanna in a gentle hug, forcing himself not to crush her like a bear the way he and Stephanos had in happier times.

She hugged back, hard, and Ængelos smiled bitterly. She would recover, if he managed not to add to her grief.

"Promise me you won't go out," Ióanna begged. "Not until your father is well enough to join you."

"I cannot," he replied and pulled away, his voice thick with womanly phlegm.

"Promise me you'll come back," Ióanna whispered as she sank against the wall separating her from her husband's sickroom, but Ængelos was already gone.

* * *

"He left?" Brithwynn asked.

"He had to," Milica replied. "The storms may be lightening here, but only because they have moved north to fall over the lands upstream of us. The levees will continue to be at risk until the flooding passes down the rivers and out to sea, and we bear responsibility for them. Pass me another bandage."

Ióanna and Magdalena should be helping to bind up the poor, broken body of Stephanos, but Ióanna could not be budged from Iakovos' bedside and Magda had withdrawn to the household chapel, there to pray for Stephanos' soul.

It was better this way. Ióanna's immense grief frightened Brithwynn and brought back her own recent loss, the only time she remembered ever seeing such deep heartache. She would help Milica do Martha's part and hope that prayers would hold off further grief.

Brithwynn passed Milica the roll of linen, then took another to wrap Stephanos' left arm. They would join Magdalena in the chapel as soon as they were done here, though she would rather find the distant chamber where Viviana and the other young women had taken the household children to keep them from disturbing the household's grief. Then she would find Rafn and find out from him exactly how this tragedy had happened.

She should probably do that first, Brithwynn realized. In the smaller households of provincial kings, it was the duty of the ladies of the house to care for the wounded, just like it was theirs to tend to the dead. She owed it to him to ensure he wasn't being forgotten in this house of grief.

* * *

It took some time to find the small chamber where Rafn had been brought. It felt strange looking in on one of her guardsmen herself, but, as Brithwynn reminded herself, this was the provinces, where delegation was a luxury few could afford.

The door was closed and unguarded, though, so Brithwynn had to shift the tray of food she carried to open the door herself.

As she did so, she heard a young female voice inside Rafn's room. Brithwynn couldn't understand her through the room's thick door, but there were few enough reasons why one of the palace women might be there.

She paused, unwilling to interrupt their private interview.

Rafn's deep rumble was easier to understand.

"No, I had no idea it was your kingdom's prince," he replied. "It was pouring down in sheets, so all I knew was that someone was slogging those bags of dirt an orguiá or so away from me. Just like someone else was slogging them on the other side. Then a tree crashed into the levee, and we were both fighting for our lives. Some others, too, unless they all dove in to save us."

Again the girl's voice was hardly audible through the door.

"Yes," Rafn replied. "Probably. But the prince was caught up in the tree, while I'd been further away and was just carried along. They couldn't pull him out until the tree hit a debris dam and stopped moving."

The girl spoke again.

"I would have, once I learned he was still in the water. But when I stood up, that's when I realized my leg was broken."

Brithwynn smiled and turned away. If this tragedy had brought Rafn to the attention of some admirer, it had some small silver lining. There was time enough to find out who she was if their attraction turned serious during their time here.

Magda hadn't eaten since yesterday. Maybe something on the tray would tempt her.

* * *

"Be my strength, sisters," Magdalena asked Brithwynn and Milica several days later, when Stephanos had been buried under a cairn of dirt and rocks on a hillside that remained a little above the floodwaters.

The once-ebullient girl Brithwynn had first met was gone, possibly forever. Like Ióanna, she walked around in a daze, her eyes red from crying even when they weren't filled with tears.

"Stephanos' parents have welcomed me far more than... than I would expect of the strangers they were, but I can't stay here," Magdalena blurted out.

"Of course not," Brithwynn said comfortingly, but the other girl continued as if she hadn't heard her.

"I can't spend the rest of my life mourning a man I was just learning to know or marry someone his parents choose to replace him, not when I could return home to my own people."

"You need us beside you when you tell them," Brithwynn understood. "You know we will."

"Glenopolis is even further from your home than it is from mine," Milica added. "And I can't imagine staying here if Ængelos were to die." She crossed herself against the possibility. "Of course I'll stand with you."

"When do you want to tell them?" Brithwynn asked.

"A hundred years ago," Magda replied through her tears. "Never."

"You can tell them now," Milica said, taking her hand, "or at least the queen."

Basilios Iakovos was on the mend, but Methodios allowed nobody but Prinkeps Ængelos and a couple servants to see him. He had little sympathy for Basilissa Ióanna's tears.

"If you're ready?"

Magdalena said nothing but followed Milica like an obedient child, though she quailed when they reached the queen's chamber and saw her. The queen was sitting in her favorite chair, staring blindly out at the rain that rippled over the small window's wavy glass.

Magdalena started backing out of the room, bumping into Brithwynn before she realized Magdalena was trying to leave.

Ióanna looked up and saw them.

"My dears, come in," she said, and Magdalena had no other choice. She knelt on the floor before Ióanna's chair, her hands seeking the older woman's before she looked up and met her eyes.

Magdalena seemed at a loss for words. She opened and closed her mouth like a fish would, but nothing came out.

Brithwynn laid a hand on Magdalena's shoulder and felt the girl shudder. Milica placed a hand on Magdalena's other shoulder and began flexing it in little cat-strokes.

Magdalena pulled her lips up into a tight little smile as she turned her head slightly to meet Brithwynn's eyes, then took a quick breath and spoke.

"I don't want to add to your sorrows, Mother," Magdalena said, her voice thick with emotion. "But with Stephanos... gone, I..." She took a deep breath. "I should return home, to my people and my father's house."

"Oh!" Basilissa Ióanna exclaimed as tears burst afresh from her reddened eyes. "Dear child, you don't have to go!"

"I know that, Mother," Magdalena replied as the tears overwhelmed her levees. "But I need to. I can't... this place was all about him to me. I need to return to my family and our home."

"Aren't we your family too?" Basilissa Ióanna moaned. "Must we lose you too?"

Magdalena buried her face in the older woman's lap as tears wracked her body. Basilissa Ióanna moaned and collapsed onto her, their tears mingling.

Brithwynn stood beside Magdalena, growing more uncomfortable as time passed and the two women before her seemed even more lost in their grief. She shifted her weight and started to step back and remove herself from their private grief.

Milica caught her eye and reached out a hand.

No, her expression said. *Stay. You're one of us.*

Brithwynn took her hand and felt her own grief burst through.

Some time later, Basilissa Ióanna pulled herself together enough to sit up and look over the three girls curled up around her knees.

"My little chicks," she whispered, her voice raw. "My poor girls."

Milica took her hand and held it lightly.

"You suffer more than any of us," she said. "He was brother or lover to us, but to you –"

Her voice caught. "I hope never to understand your pain!"

"Age brings a certain wisdom, my child," Basilissa Ióanna said, a bittersweet smile breaking through her tears. "I know I'll one day be glad for the pain, because of the joy it followed. And I know I'll see him again, in a world where all pain is forgotten in a never-ending joy. But until then, we must continue as we can."

"And that often means more loss," she said, turning her attention back to Magdalena. "Although I have no wish to ever see you go, my child. And you will always – *always* – have a home here. For Stephanos and for your own self. How long will you stay?"

"I..." she paused. "I don't know. I just know I need to go home."

"Stay till winter is past," Milica suggested. "It's too late in the season to sail even if you left today, and I'm not sure you could make the journey any other way."

"True," Magdalena replied. "The mountain passes are surely closed."

She blinked away the tears that weighed down her lashes.

"I can stay till spring," she said. "I have to, don't I? It will give me time... to say goodbye."

"That could take forever," Milica said.

"No," Basilissa Ióanna said. "Too long a goodbye is as bad as too short of one. Stay till spring, and you'll know if you still need to leave."

"Yes, Mother," Magdalena replied. "I'll stay till spring. Brithwynn may even leave before I do."

"Reminding me that I'm losing both of you so soon?" Basilissa Ióanna chided Magdalena, though her voice had some of its old spirit back.

"No!" Magdalena whispered, glancing over her shoulder at Brithwynn. "I didn't mean – I only –"

"All is well, my dear," Basilissa Ióanna shushed her. "Life is about loss, and finding the strength to continue despite it. Losing two of my girls back to your families is no loss at all compared to what we've lost together."

Brithwynn wished she had family waiting for her at the end of her journey.

* * *

"If the gods had given me another son," Basilissa Ióanna said, clapping both Brithwynn's hands as if she never wanted to let go, "I'd want him to marry you."

"If you had, I'd want the same," Brithwynn replied, surprising herself with the fervency with which she meant it. It was hard to believe she'd met them less than a month ago.

"You will always be like a daughter to me," Ióanna half-whispered to Brithwynn, hugging her close. "And you'll *always* be welcome here."

"There she goes," Iakovos chuckled, though he still looked pale and weak after his illness, "adopting every noble maiden who wanders past. But our gates are always open for you, and a warm place by the fire."

Brithwynn hugged them both, surprising Iakovos, who grunted in surprise. For that matter, she surprised herself. Familial affection hadn't exactly been a significant part of life in the Blachernai, at least not after her mother died.

Magdalena and Milica hugged her tight even before she turned around.

"I wish you could stay," Milica whispered.

So did Brithwynn, though she felt she'd put her Glenabenian family in too much danger already. If she'd stayed till spring, it would be even harder to say goodbye – if Ióannés' people hadn't found her by then.

She couldn't take the chance that she would bring more grief to this family.

"Pray for me, sister," Magdalena asked as she squeezed her tight. "And be safe."

"You too," Brithwynn replied. "Both of you. And come see me if you're ever in Trimaria!"

"We will!" both girls replied, though Brithwynn doubted that Magda would ever be closer to Trimaria than she was now. Her homeland of Dalmatia lay too far to the west.

"And come see us next time you're in Glenabenia," Milica added.

Brithwynn hugged both girls again and turned to climb into her saddle. As she adjusted the skirt of her simple wool gown, she looked up and smiled.

Rafn seemed quite taken with his silver lining. His young bride looked around nervously from her saddle as he withdrew from her ever so slowly to take his accustomed place with the guard.

4

The River Road

The hills along the Volkhov River were a blur of white through the softly-falling snow, but that didn't stop the river from living up to its name. The Volkhov was always a meeting place, but it was at its busiest in early spring and late fall, when eager traders set out for distant markets or made their slow way home, laden with bright coin and goods from distant lands.

Their oxen plodded slowly over the frozen river, but it was still better to travel this way than wait until May or June for the river to become passable by boat. Its wide expanse was filled with longboats on wooden runners and simple sledges, both theirs and those of travelers from many other Rús settlements, most intent on reaching their desired markets before too many of their competition. Like them, many of the other travelers they passed had stripped their boats down to only the tar-sealed shell in order to load them high with as much as the oxen could pull, raised them up onto slick wooden runners, then used the rest of the boats' seasoned wood to make simple sledges, the rafts of the ice roads, that could perhaps carry a few more items.

There was scarcely space for anyone to ride, but that was what skis were for.

The short early-spring days passed in rapid progress up the broad expanse of ice-road. Occasionally, Baldar or one of the other chieftains would set aside their skis to clamber up on a ship or sledge to talk business with one or more of their companions – and enough mead to sail on.

This was the life!

The forests along the Volkhov still came up to the edge of the frozen river for much of its length, but centuries of constant trade along the river had created periodic clearings along it, often with rudimentary improvements to make them more convenient waystations for the traders who made the river their home.

As dusk began to fall, each chieftain and his men guided their sledges over to a suitable-looking stretch of riverbank, jostling for one of the better sites when they could and clearing enough space for their einherjars to camp for a night or two along the riverbank. Before full dark, the aromas of cooking foods and the sounds of feasting and com-petitions of strength or fighting ability lay thick over the white woods. Nights of bitter cold still kept them huddled close in their temporary shelters, but as they made their way up the Volkhov, winter loosened its grip on the land enough that many of the men filled their nights with drinking and games of prowess by firelight.

* * *

The wood-walled city appeared out of the drifting snow like the dwelling-place of ghosts, though the sounds that carried through the cold air gave proof that it belonged in the land of the living. Before long, they could hear men shouting along the city's great docks that bordered both sides of the river.

Ahead of them, the first ships' oxen pulled them up close to the quieter dock on the south side of the river, where the prince and most of the city's elite lived in the shadow of the great new cathedral of St Sofia.

Arnfastr took one look at the dock and swung out past the crowd of ships waiting for a spot next to it. Any man who couldn't leap from ship to ship at dock was no true vikingr, and he wasn't about to wait around for a space by the docks when he could make his own space. Other ship-masters followed him, and before long, a man could leap from one side of the frozen river to the other without touching foot to the ice.

By then, he had leapt down from the ship that rested between his ship and the shore – one of the Bjornsfolk, who were tossing host-gifts and other things to their folk on the dock below – and dropped onto the ice-covered dock. Its liberal covering of ashes and small tree limbs seemed to have been reapplied sometime that day.

Good. Ash-mix made for a better footing than a sheet of ice, though there probably wouldn't be a good excuse for a real fight while they were here. He'd wait in comfort for his thralls to bring his host-gifts while he was enjoying a roaring fire and someone else's mead.

* * *

Munin carried Baldar back to his youth at the sight of the great city of Holmgarðr, chief city in the rich river-land of Gardariki. Here, his father had sent him with the small einherjar that was all he could spare from Vinka, so many years ago. The city and palace of great spruce logs had seemed so vast when he'd first come here, a small, scrawny boy of twelve, with a puppy's oversized hands and feet, elbows and knees that stuck out everywhere, and ears that protruded from his thatch of brown hair.

It had seemed even larger when filled with the knyaz' own sons and the men of their einherjars, brave princelings and strong men well-grown in height and ferocity, men like his eldest brother Ranulf and his men. But these men had taken him in and taught him all he knew of kingship and trade along the riverways. They had led him in battle and taught him the ways of women. And when the old king, Knyaz Ruric, had died in his bed and some of the minor lords had rebelled, Baldar had ridden as a brother with Alric and his closest brothers and companions to bring the rebellious lords back under Holmgarðr's sway. When the fighting was done, he'd been rewarded like the true brother he was.

That had been the beginning of Àsgarðr.

* * *

The young man looked like Þór.

"You remember my eldest son, Grimar?" Knyaz Alric of Gardariki said, his voice thick with pride.

"He's grown since I last saw him," Baldar said, putting out his arm in greeting.

Young Grimar took his forearm with confidence and a firm grip, without trying to make it a wrestling match.

He didn't need to. As young as he was, Grimar carried his weapons with the surety that comes only from skilled use. He looked unwounded.

Little Ásaka could have chosen him for his looks alone, but Baldar had more important things to consider.

"Your father tells me you've grown into a strong young man," Baldar said, sitting on the well-furred chair Alric's people had placed beside his low throne and taking up his horn of mead.

"A strong man brags not, but lets his deeds speak for him," Grimar said. "Yet I give the skalds enough to sing of."

"More than enough!" Alric bragged. "You heard of the skrælings that attacked the city of Beloozero on the Sheksna? Of course you have! It was my Grimar who rode there with his men in time to slay every skræling and save those of its people who were left. Then he held it while his men helped rebuild the city's walls better than before and defended it until enough of its men had returned to hold it themselves."

"He did well the work of a prince," Baldar agreed. "And how many Grimarlingas did you leave to strengthen their defense in future years?"

"A couple tylpt, Good Father," Grimar replied with a grin, "and my men at least as many. The fields were ready to be plowed."

Baldar felt Munin stretch his cheeks with memories from his youth. "You make the people strong, boy. But my Ásaka will never be faced with an älskare or her offspring under her roof, nor will either replace her or her princelings. If you ever choose one of them in place of her and hers, if you even give her cause to leave you, you will pay her her weight in wifgelðr and let her return to the home of her mother."

"I would never dishonor her like that." Grimar declared.

"Nor in any other way," Alric added. "Else it will be *three* times her weight in gold. And it will be her weight at the time, with all the padding her children gave her, not her weight now as a slip of a girl. You'll have every reason to make this marriage a success."

"I need no more reason to love her than that she is the daughter of my father's friend and said to be as beautiful as her mother," Grimar said. "But I will add that she must be wearing all the jewelry and furs I will have given her if she ever needs this weighing. And I will start my wif-gifts with a pair of brooches that I will send north with the messenger who informs her that we are agreed to be wed. On our wedding night, I will give her a chunk of amber no smaller than my thumb, on a chain with pearls and lapis. Then she will know that she is loved as my true wife."

Alric nodded and smiled.

"When I have passed to Valhalla and young Grimar has replaced me on the Holmgarðr throne, your Ásaka will be queen of all the lands of the Gardariki, from Staraya Ladoga to Gnezdovo and as much further as we expand our territory by then. Her sons will each rule one of the greatest cities of the Gardariki and govern its trade until the eldest replaces Grimar on the throne in turn and raises his brothers as high as he can. Her daughters will be married to the best and strongest of our allies, where they shall become queens in turn."

"You honor me too much, brother," Baldar grinned at Alric and Grimar. "And you, my son!"

"This marriage will be a blessing to both our families, brother," Alric said, leaning back against the high back of his chair with satisfaction. "But I would ask one favor of you."

"If it lies within my power," Baldar replied, feeling no less satisfied by their decision.

"My third son," Alric said. "Þórbranðr, he's nearly fifteen summers now and I have too little to give him, too few men or ships after I give his brothers enough to get them started. And I have no men as skilled as you to mentor him in the ways of the world."

"It's the curse of the third son," Baldar said ruefully. For every third son like himself who built a better life for himself in a place like Asgarðr, many more must surely fail or barely scrape by.

"I forgot," Alric said, looking up sharply. "You're a third son."

Baldar doubted that his friend had forgotten, though he was more interested in what he was getting at.

He shrugged. "It is what it is."

"I have men enough who will follow him," Alric continued, "but not men enough to send him out into the world with no guidance. I would send him out with you, under your guidance."

"And you would have him learn from me, so he makes the connections I can give him down among the Bysantinski."

"Yes, brother," Alric replied. "I can help him here, but you can help him more in Mikligarðr or this Trimaria."

"You know he's welcome," Baldar replied. If this boy Þórbranðr was anything like his older brother, Alric was doing him a favor. If he wasn't, the boy wouldn't be the first piece of raw iron he'd worked into shape.

"I'll get him started," Baldar agreed. "Where he goes from there will be up to him."

* * *

Baldar was feeling very mellow by the time Alric's men and those of his elder sons' einherjars began to troop in for the evening meal. Several of Knyaginya Marina's young women came in with horns of Marina's honey mead, which they carried around as Marina or Alric gestured.

His first älskare had been one of those girls, a niece of the old king. She'd meant the world to him, at least until her parents had arranged her marriage to a prince among the Slavs. Last he'd heard, she had a boatload of children and would be a grandmother soon.

Baldar sighed. Some of those beauties could be her daughters.

He shouldn't think about that. Too much time spent thinking about past loves turned a man off future ones, and a woman was as good as three dogs when it comes to warming a man's bed and made for much better company... at least usually. He hoped to be at least as old as Snorri before he lost his taste for them, or his ability to please them when it counted.

More women came into the hall, carrying trays full of roasted meats and bread that smelled like it had just come from the ovens. Two of them carried their trays up to the table and placed them before Baldar and Alric, who cut a large chunk of meat and placed it before Baldar before cutting another for himself and Marina.

Life was good.

Baldar had eaten the first chunk of meat and helped himself to another when Alric stood and gestured at one of the boys sitting down by the far end of the crowd.

"You've not met my Þórbranðr since he was a mewling babe," Alric said, as the boy stood and strode up to the table.

Baldar was sure he had, if only by a handful of years. But the boy had grown since then, even if he hadn't grown enough to look like a man yet. Young Þórbranðr Alricssen had yet to grow his first chin hair. If he turned sideways, he could still probably hide behind a birch sapling.

He had a long way to go till he reached his brother's stature, if he ever did.

But Baldar could work with that. He'd been that.

And the boy had a sizeable einherjar. That in itself was a good marriage gift, though the boy would take it with him when he eventually struck out on his own.

"Baldar Langstriter hertogi," he said, putting his arm out across the table to clasp the boy's. "Of Asgarðr."

"Þórbranr Alricssen Knyazhich," the boy said, clasping his arm firmly enough. "My father told me all about you."

He might be thin, but he had muscles like grapevines.

"Hopefully not just the trouble we got up to," Baldar said, winking at Alric.

"Oh, no sir," Þórbranðr replied. "Faðir said you were the best man to finish my training."

"He would know," Baldar laughed. "I finished his training, when he was still wet behind the ears."

"What lies are you telling my son?" Alric rumbled from behind his drinking horn. "I finished your training, boy!"

"Who taught you to drink till you saw Lady Sól drive Alsviðr and Árvakr up into the sky?" Baldar asked Alric.

"And who taught you that maids can make a man feel like Odin?" Alric replied.

"What! Old and half-blind?"

"No, fool! Like he's surrounded by Valkyries!"

"You have the right of it, then, my brother," Baldar replied, lifting his horn to Alric in acknowledgement. "You finished my training, you half-blind old fool!"

Alric slammed his drinking horn into Baldar's so hard the mead splashed onto the table and laughed uproariously, while Þórbranðr looked from one old fool to the other as if he'd never seen them before.

Baldar raised his drinking horn, his eyes on the shields and torches that hung heavy on the strong walls of Alric's longhall.

All this would be Ásaka's soon. Or soon enough, with the turning of the world and a few years' guidance from Alric's Marina, who was surely a good woman if no match for his Ása. And with it the eldest scion of the powerful Rurikid family.

It was even a better match than he'd gotten for Eden. He and his people had truly arrived.

* * *

The Lovat stretched away, wide and flat before them, as it had been since they left Holmgarðr and crossed the frozen length of Lake Ilmen. The near-constant snows that had followed them nearly to Holmgarðr had parted, leaving the world gleaming in its crystalline glory beneath a sky the color of lapis.

"This is what men were made for," Ædrick said expansively, throwing his arms open to take in the whole world in its frozen glory. "To travel, to fight, and to see new sights around every bend of the river!"

"And every night, to feast like Odin's einherjar do in Valhalla," Bjorn agreed.

"Ja, vol! The river road, it is Valhalla!"

"I could make these sledges faster, I think," Bjorn said a few minutes later, as the icy landscape sped past.

"How much faster could you want to go?" Ædrick asked. "Faster than Þór?"

"Maybe not faster than the old hammer-swinger. But fast as lightning, sure, that would be a challenge worth accepting! Would you work with me, brother?"

"I would! What have you tried?"

"Naught yet. But the runners stick worst in the morning, when they've been sitting all night. I would try some of the pitch we use on the boats and see if that will seal them enough that they don't stick. Then the oxen won't have to pull so hard to get them going."

"I can help you next long camp, brother," Ædrick said. "Or once we have everything."

"No worries, brother," Bjorn said. "I brought enough pitch for a tylpt new boats. We just need a long camp in a place with many trees, and we'll get this sledge as fast as oxen can pull it."

"Oxen are slow beasts," Ædrick said after watching the trees pass on either side. "You'd need horses to get much faster, or maybe goats or cats. We have few horses and no goats or cats that could pull a sledge."

"We'll have to get some, then. I've a mind to race Þór."

* * *

Vikarr nudged Hafgrimr and stared at the boy who was walking purposefully toward their campfire.

"You seek someone?" he called out.

The boy stopped, taking up a position just outside the circle of firelight. He stood, his legs spread and his hands on his hips, looking them up and down like a clan chieftain who needed to man his boats but doubted they'd be worth their bread.

Valkyries take such young striplings, or take him before he had to answer to them!

"You, if you're Vikarr Bjornssen," he said.

"What do you want with Vikarr?" Hafgrimr growled. The younger Bjornssen hadn't thought much of such striplings since they were striplings themselves. Or maybe it was the air of a princeling he carried. A child had no place carrying himself like a king. This one looked like the boy old Alric had given to Baldar at the feast before they'd left Holmgarðr, so maybe he thought he was a king.

"The Hertogi said to ask you to show me where to have my men camp this night, and to teach me your ways."

"A little wet behind the ears, aren't you?" Vikarr growled. "What are you doing out on the river without your wet-nurse?"

"This is my third season," the boy replied, his voice firm despite his youth.

"Three whole summers!" Hafgrimr barked. "Hear that, boys?"

"You're no man till you've been out six seasons," Dálkr drawled. "I've a son been out nearly that long."

"Sure he's yours?" Udvarhelyi laughed. "Seems you were gone an awful lot that summer, and the herdsmen had plenty of time to start looking good."

"He's mine." Dálkr said proudly. "Have you seen his flaming hair and broad shoulders? He looks just like I did at his age."

"All settled, then. He's definitely the herdsman's. That man's twice your size."

The boy groaned audibly, drawing every eye back to him.

"You want a nursemaid, boy?" Vikarr demanded.

"Never," the boy said. "I want nothing but to join the army of the great Baldar Langstriter Hertogi until I can take my men out into the world on my own."

"You want a nursemaid," Hafgrimr said.

"I want a fight. Against you or beside you, you decide. Unless you take too long."

"I'll see what we can do for you, princeling." Vikarr bowed, mockingly echoing the southern forms. "Till then, you and yours can camp over there."

He pointed to an open space a bit further down the slope toward the Lovat.

"I trust we don't have to show you how to set up your camp, since you've been out for three seasons."

* * *

Bjorn laughed into the wind.

"Can you believe it?" he asked. "This has got to be the fastest men have ever traveled!"

Ædrick grinned, looking out at the frozen landscape.

"And now we know why Þór travels all the world!" he said. "Who would not when this is what he sees, from a chariot that flies as fast as eagles?"

* * *

"Well met, kinsmen!" a Vitebski Rús yelled out to them as Baldar's first ships approached the rough wooden dock, longer even than the docks Ástríðr had seen in Holmgarð. Though ships lined more than half their length, there was still space enough for seven or eight of their ships. "Who comes to share food and fire with Prince Radhger of Vitebsk?

"I do," Baldar called out, stepping up onto the prow of the ship and throwing back his fur-lined cloak to show off the gold and amber that marked him as a king among their people. "Baldar Langstriter, lord of Asgarðr and leader of these men. We sail to Bysantinsk."

"Riches come on such a journey!" the man grinned widely at him. "Our lord welcomes you and yours to hall and board in great Vitebsk!"

Three of his men tossed ropes out to the men on the dock, and the Vitebski spokesman took up one of them, pulling it in and lashing the ship securely to the dock. Behind them, other Vitebski helped more of Baldar's ships tie up.

Baldar dropped onto the dock and stepped forward to clasp the Vitebski's arm in his. "We bring gifts and good foods to share with your master, my friend."

Behind him, Eiríkr and Lundvarr unloaded the chests of amber and arctic furs that had been set aside as a gift for this high lord among the Rus.

* * *

"What news from the river-road, brother?" Baldar asked Radhger. Before them, their men pitted themselves against each other in friendly competition as the longhouse rang with their boasting and course laughter. Many betted on whether Dálkr or Radhger's man Sven would best the other in their wrestling match beside the hearth.

"Traders talk of a new tribe of skrælings attacking river traffic. Not having numbers to attack the walled Empire cities, they rove the wastes between the rivers and carry off what they can take from weak villages and careless traders."

"Tell true! Where hunt they?"

"Hear now they've crossed the Volga. The Don they now hunt, none others yet as we've heard."

"Skrælings strike fear in the hearts of our kin, not merely those of the Empire?"

"Few fear until encountered they are, yet many after. None yet can stand against them save behind stone walls."

"Good would such a battle be, between our men and theirs. Have any yet offered yours such pleasant pastime?"

"None yet, though many seek them. We venture not unasked into the lands beyond the Desna, where our brothers of Atlantia rule for the distant Emperor."

"Perhaps before they take us, the gods to us will send such fearsome play."

"Would that they will, my brother!" Radhger thrust his horn toward the rafters. "Would that they will! But what brings you this far south before the spring thaws?"

"A summons," Baldar said. "And an offer. You've heard about the Mikligarðr emperor?"

"If well I've heard, he fell to poison in the fall."

"T'is true," Baldar said. "The dróttning his daughter summoned me to help her hold her lands."

"A Mikligarðr princess summoned you to the Empire?" Knyaz Radhger of Vitebsk slapped Baldar soundly on the back. "The gods must love you... or hate you."

"Ja, vol," Baldar laughed. "As long as they know my name."

"True, brother! What more could a man want, than that and plenty of mead?"

"Women!" Baldar laughed, throwing his head back. "Fighting, mead, and women, till the gods summon us to Valhalla!"

"I'll drink to that, brother!"

5

Meridia

"You have a choice to make, Princess," Valgarðr said. "Ióannésopo-lis, the capital of Meridia, lies ahead of us about a day's journey."

"And?"

"And they are surely awaiting us, after everything that happened in Glenopolis. But there's the possibility that we'll be walking into a trap if any spies in Glenopolis have realized who you really are. We can avoid that risk if we leave the main road and take back ways to the city of Arenopolis at the mouth of the Dnieper, but that could set off another set of problems if our friends here think you've encountered brigands or decide you're not who you claimed to be and send troops after you."

"And since I'm not, not really..."

"That could be trouble," Valgarðr concluded. "Especially since we'd probably have trouble differentiating between our friends and enemies who want to deliver you to Ióannés."

"I suppose once I travel openly as anyone worth mentioning, it's the only real choice I have."

"Not quite," Valgarðr replied. "Remember, I can always make you disappear if you need me to. But we should save that for if we know someone's after you."

"So I'm Eiríni again," Brithwynn said.

"Once more," Valgarðr replied. "Once more, and you are home."

* * *

Ióannésopolis turned out to be much bigger than it had first appeared to be, spread out as it was across three hills. Its gates stood open the next day, a bright, clear fall day that belied the foul weather they had encountered in Glenopolis. Even from a distance, Brithwynn could see the crowds of people coming and going from the city.

The main boulevard in Ióannésopolis was nearly as narrow and crooked as the one in Glenopolis, but it felt even more crowded. Throngs of people seemed intent on conducting much of their business in the middle of the street or tried to squeeze past on their way to wherever they were going. Their passage was made all the more difficult because the boulevard seemed to follow every little turn of what had once been a creekbed between the city's hills, though the creek had apparently been tamed and used to supply water to the fountains in every plaza and courtyard they passed.

This is truly an Imperial city, Brithwynn thought. Each grand public building they passed proclaimed its purpose to any who understood the codes of proper Rhōmaiōn architecture, and the private dwellings announced the status of their owners in the same way.

If she looked closely, she could see signs of the improvements each had undergone at least once in the course of the city's growth from a simple tribal town to a regional capital of the Empire.

Brithwynn had often admired Constantinopolis's architecture as a way to liven up the boredom of a slow palanquin ride through the city, and it felt almost like she was back there, on her way perhaps to the Hagia Sophia or to the Old Palace.

But the crowds!

Brithwynn had never had trouble passing through the streets of Constantinopolis, thanks in no small part to the heralds and guards who always preceded and surrounded her imperial palanquin. Even when she'd escaped Constantinopolis dressed as a servant, the early-morning hour had kept the traffic relatively light.

But now the crowds seemed to press in on her, slowing her party and making it harder for them to remain together. Valgarðr and Kormákr still flanked her, but the rest of her party stretched out far behind them in the narrow streets, making even Valgarðr somewhat unsettled. Though he gave a fair impression of riding as confidently as he had out on the road, Brithwynn kept noticing him exchanging glances with Brendan or one of the other Varangians who rode close behind her.

Despite Glenopolis, Brithwynn felt her nerves grow tight.

"Tell me about these people," she asked Valgarðr.

Valgarðr looked around. "You can probably see the imperial influence."

He smiled tightly as Brithwynn nodded.

"Meridia was founded by Rús traders who travelled south to trade at the mouth of the Dnieper, near where Arenopolis is now. Since most of their trade was with the Empire, they quickly became civilized. Their first king, Oleg, was baptized in the 6367th year of the world and took the Christian name Ióannés. Since then, they've had increasingly close ties to the Empire and officially came under the Aegis Rhōmaiōn with the marriage of the Imperial Princess Juliana Komnena to the Meridian Sebastokrator Gavriil, just over a century ago."

"So their royal family are actually my cousins?"

"Twice over," Valgarðr replied. "Remember, they come from the same branch of the Rús that your mother's family came from, as does the Glenabenian royal family."

"So they're trustworthy?"

"Absolutely."

"Then why do you keep looking around like that?"

"Because I've never liked to be closed in like this, and there's always a chance your cousins aren't the ones in charge up there anymore. Meridia is a bigger target than Glenabenia, and Basilios Timofei has certainly been approached by at least one of the contenders for the Eternal Throne. He might have been required to take a side, or possibly even replaced with someone who would."

"Then why did we come here?" Brithwynn exclaimed, pulling on the reins so Iphigenia stopped abruptly.

"Because we need to know what the situation is, and this is our best place to find out what we need to know," Valgarðr replied in a rough-voiced whisper barely loud enough for her to hear.

"And the danger to Eiríni is negligible," he added, leaving unsaid the danger they would all face if anyone were to learn her real name.

"Even if the king's been forced to take a side?"

"Even then," Valgardr replied. "I just don't like not knowing."

Brithwynn eased up on the reins, allowing Iphigenia to continue her slow canter through the city. It was disconcerting – to say the least! – to find that anything about Ióannésopolis disturbed Valgarðr, but she had to trust his judgment.

He'd gotten her this far.

And they had arrived. Nearly.

A final turn of the boulevard revealed a large field, as the brick and marble valley they had been riding through opened up. Some of the soldiers of Ióannésopolis practiced their small-unit tactics on the Campus Martius, overseen by an assortment of citizens and sheep who relaxed or grazed under the trees that bordered it. Beyond the Campus, the tallest of the city's three hills overflowed with the regal-looking homes of its wealthiest inhabitants.

Somewhere up there was the Meridian royal palace, where they would soon be expected – if they weren't already.

It was time to find out if Valgarðr was right to worry.

* * *

Bold black-and-white banners hung from the whitewashed stone towers of the Meridian royal palace, rippling in the crisp fall air. Before them, a small royal party awaited her on the palace steps.

Brithwynn rode up to where a cluster of grooms awaited her party, almost midway between the palace and the small plaza where the central boulevard terminated in front of the palace. She dismounted, allowing the grooms to lower her gently to the ground instead of dropping lightly, the way she preferred to dismount when there was nobody around to see except her own people.

This wouldn't make Verina groan.

Most of her younger ladies dismounted on their own instead of waiting for the grooms to help them down, while the Varangians dismounted with the ease of long practice. She waited a few moments, long enough for the grooms to help Verina and Ismenia down from their horses, then stepped forward toward the royal party.

Her ladies walked close behind her as she approached. Though she didn't look, she knew that Valgarðr kept his Varangians back far enough that they wouldn't be an overt threat.

The king stepped forward as Brithwynn approached, coming to the lowest step of the palace. Tall and broad, he resembled her brother Ióannés, or Stephanos before the accident.

She performed a simple obeisance at about an orguiá away, like those she had seen at Iakovos' court.

As she rose, she noticed that the king had closed the distance between them. He took her hands in his and helped her to her feet.

"My brother Iakovos of Glenabenia sent me word that you would be visiting us on your way home, Kyria Eirini," he said.

"Your welcome is most appreciated," Brithwynn replied.

"My wife and daughter join me in offering you the hospitality of our house," he said, turning to indicate the queen and a princess only a couple years younger than Brithwynn. "The lovely Basilissa Epiphania and Prinkepissa Domentzia of Meridia."

The two stepped forward, and Brithwynn found herself looking the princess in her eyes, which twinkled mischievously.

"Have you come to spend the feast of the Theotokos with us?" she asked.

"I... I don't know, Prinkepissa," Brithwynn replied. "It's almost a fortnight away."

"Of course she is," Basilissa Epiphania said.

Turning to Brithwynn, she added, "Unless you need to leave us before then?"

Did they have two weeks? Brithwynn had only hoped they could stay through the end of the week.

"My lady," Verina interjected, stepping forward, "We'll still reach the Dnieper before the winter storms close it if we celebrate the feast of the Theotokos here."

She paused. "And these old bones could use the break."

"You're not old!" Brithwynn exclaimed, as Basilissa Epiphania smiled broadly.

"We're so glad you're staying through the holiday," she said.

* * *

The Meridian royal palace seemed almost twice the size of the Glenabenian one and was built entirely of stone, though the Blachernai still dwarfed it. Like the Glenabenian palace, its throne room was also the main hall, though a wide balcony running along three sides of it opened up the space and allowed many more people to gather there. More black and white banners hung from the great pillars supporting the balcony and made the ceiling feel far beyond human reach.

It almost felt like the Blachernai. A smaller version of it, anyway.

"I must apologize for my daughter," Basilissa Epiphania said as they walked toward the dais and the great stone hearth where a small fire burned. "Prinkepissa Domentzia has been excited about your visit ever since the pigeon arrived with Basilios Iakovos' message."

She glanced back at her daughter and smiled fondly. "She's met the Glenabenian Prinkepissaes a couple times and decided that any friend of theirs is certain to be a friend of hers."

"I hope so, too," Brithwynn said, smiling at the girl.

"She also hopes you'll tell us – her especially – about your travels," Basilios Timofei said, his tone mock-severe. "Not that I'd mind some fresh news from beyond our borders, mind you. But Domentzia will pester you night and day for 'one more story' from your travels."

"Except when she's trying to get you to climb trees with her," Basilissa Epiphania added. "I swear, the girl tries to climb high enough to see Constantinopolis!"

"And we're harvesting apples again this week!" Domentzia grinned.

"You don't have to help," Basilissa Epiphania told Brithwynn. "And you certainly don't have to climb trees with her, regardless of how she might try to convince you."

"I'll try to remember that," Brithwynn said, unsure whether it would give away her secret if she were to admit that she'd never climbed a tree.

"We have a few rooms ready for you and your people," Basilissa Epiphania said. "Upstairs for you and your ladies, down with our guards for any of yours not guarding your door. I hope they'll be satisfactory, but I have to warn you. Domentzia insisted that yours be beside hers."

Brithwynn laughed. "How else are we to become friends?"

"Domentzia will show you your room," Basilios Timofei said, his face growing serious. "But first, I have a question for you."

He gestured her over to the low Rús thrones that dominated the dais, even though they were scarcely bigger or more elaborate than the regular chairs around them.

He sat on one of the thrones and gestured Brithwynn to one of the surrounding chairs before continuing.

"My brother Glenabenia tells me you were with them when tragedy struck his court."

Brithwynn felt her heart's blood sink. Had he gotten the misapprehension that she was somehow the reason for Stephanos' death?

"Yes, my lord," she replied, her heart in her throat. "I was visiting them, though I wasn't out by the levée when it happened."

"I didn't think you were," he replied. "But Basilios Iakovos tells me your men were out there with his. Is there anything you can tell me that he might not have known... or been willing to trust to a bird that might be shot down or captured?"

What could he mean?

What did he fear?

"I had never before seen a drowned body," she said, hoping that her small amount of knowledge was enough. "But I saw no reason to doubt what Basilios Iakovos and his men said happened, especially since my own men related the same events."

"One of my own men also fell into the river when the levee gave way," she added, certain that Basilios Timofei knew or would soon learn of Rafn's narrow escape.

She didn't want to appear to be holding anything back.

"Your man Rafn," he nodded, and Brithwynn was glad she'd mentioned him.

"The one with his leg in a splint and a pretty girl helping him?"

"The very same. Basina joined us in Glenopolis."

"O-ho, a bedside romance!" Basilios Timofei laughed. "Marry the nurse, that's the idea!"

"She's been a blessing," Brithwynn replied somewhat stiffly, not sure how to take the king's course-sounding comment.

"I'm sure she has," the king replied, laughter in his eyes. "And I wish them many healthy children. But for now, I should return you to my own."

* * *

The cool winds of November blew through the apple orchard, almost as chilly as the coldest January winter Brithwynn could remember in Constantinopolis. It reminded her abruptly that it had only been three months since her father died.

No. Since he was *murdered*. Assassinated by someone in his own family.

So much had changed since then. Like this, Brithwynn thought. Back in the Blachernai, she would never be wearing an old linen kamision – not even a woolen dalmatikion – and breeches to help pick the last of the apples. But here, Basilios Timofei's people made it something of a festival, where everyone in the city seemed to be helping in some way.

"Do you help your people with the harvest?" Domentzia asked, dropping another handful of apples into the cloth Brithwynn and Ariadne held stretched out below her. "Back home in Trimaria?"

"My father and brothers do," Brithwynn replied, thinking of Iakovos and his sons and wishing – not for the first time – that they were more to her than the models for "Eiríni's" family. "But I haven't, so I'm glad to be down here on the ground."

"You don't know how to climb a tree?" Domentzia asked, leaning out over a nearby tree branch to look at her directly. "A child could climb most of these! I've been doing it since I was two cubits tall."

"Here," she added, looking over at the other girl in the tree, a Meridian Brithwynn had only met at sunrise that morning. "Isidora, climb down and trade places with Eiríni for a bit."

"But I –" Brithwynn started to argue as Isidora turned and started climbing down the tree. It didn't take long.

"Nonsense!" Domentzia laughed. "See how easily Isidora got down? It's just as easy going up. Easier, maybe. And we'll get you back on the ground before we go for the last apples at the tippy top."

The thought made Brithwynn blanche. An older cousin had mysteriously died in a fall not much greater than that when she was five. The little she had seen had given her nightmares for weeks, if not months.

But she couldn't tell Domentzia that. And if a child could climb this tree...

She stepped forward, trying to gauge the last couple branches Isidora had stepped on as she came down. They kind of resembled the steps she'd used them as.

"Tuck your skirt up in your belt so it doesn't get in your way," Domentzia called down. "Isidora, help her please. And don't worry. I'll tell you what to do, every step of the way."

* * *

"You know what these always make me think of?" Domentzia asked a couple hours later as she dropped two more apples into the cloth Isidora and Ariadne held tight below them.

"No," Brithwynn replied, climbing up a little higher to reach an apple that hung just out of reach. It was actually a fun challenge, figuring out how to reach some of the higher apples.

As long as she didn't accidentally look past her feet at the ground, nearly two stories below. The first time she did that, she'd nearly lost her grip on the branch beside her. Then she'd been unable to *loosen* her grip on it.

But now she was comfortable enough in the trees that it was starting to be fun. Especially when the late fall sun warmed the fruit and the voices of birds and people alike.

"Remember the story of Atalanta?" Domentzia asked.

"The girl who decided who to marry by running a footrace against her suitors?" Brithwynn asked. "Didn't she and her husband end up getting turned into lions because she let him get carried away and mate with her in the temple?"

"She got stupid when she let him win," Domentzia judged. "But before then, she had the right idea. Marry a man who's better at something important than you are, and you've always got him either beside you or in front of you."

"But a *footrace*?" Brithwynn asked. "That seems like an awfully... petty choice of skills to choose for."

"Not as much as you think," Domentzia said. "She was a warrior, back when our people were pagans who let women fight. And back then, everyone ran into battle, not just the lowest ranks. Papa says so."

"So that footrace was more than just a footrace," Brithwynn mused.

"Right. It was a test of their martial skills," Domentzia said. "And *that's* why she killed the losers. They weren't going to fight *beside* her, so she needed to make sure they didn't fight *against* her."

"Wow! That's harsh!"

"Harsh times call for harsh actions." Domentzia sounded like she was quoting her father.

"So why did she let him distract her with the apples?"

"That's what I don't understand," Domentzia said, pausing for a moment as if she needed to focus all her attention on the apple she was picking right then. "If the footrace was only important as a facet of his martial ability, maybe she noticed something about him that made him worth losing to. Or maybe there was something really special about those apples, and they weren't really apples or even oranges."

"Or maybe the story's been changed over time to make it a parable like in Æsop's *Fables* or the ones Jesus told in the *Bible*, and that's why that part doesn't make sense."

Domentzia made a face.

"So someone turned Atalanta's footrace into a parable for how easily women can be distracted?"

"Or anyone, I suppose," Brithwynn replied. "Just because something's flashy doesn't mean it's worth losing the race."

Domentzia thought about it for a few moments before replying.

"That's a good thing to remember even if it's not what they were trying to tell people," she said. "But the man I marry will at *least* have to outrun me. And he'd better not try to trick me with a handful of apples."

"Won't you have to marry whomever your father chooses for you?" Brithwynn asked. "What if he's old and fat?"

"Papa won't choose someone who's old and fat," she said confidently. "He needs to be able to lead my armies and his, and he can't do that if he's too old or fat."

"And even if Papa did," she added with the look of someone who wouldn't hear of anyone countermanding her decision, "I'll just send him back where he came from. Wouldn't you?"

"I never really thought about it," Brithwynn replied. "I always just thought I wouldn't have a choice."

"You *always* have a choice," Domentzia declared. "You just have to have the determination to stand by your decisions."

Brithwynn winced at the naïveté she heard in the girl's claim.

"I hope you find everything you're looking for," she said, trying not to imagine how many of her siblings and other relatives would now be Augoustos or Autokratera of the Empire if winning the Eternal Thone only took some determination.

If that were all it took, Papa would still be alive. She would never have seen the outskirts of Constantinopolis, let alone the outskirts of the Empire.

* * *

Brithwynn sprawled with Domentzia and the other girls on a pile of pillows some servants had placed at one end of the huge pavilion of white wool that shaded the harvesters' luncheon.

She stretched languorously, well aware that many of her fellow harvesters were napping in the crisp fall afternoon. Viviana, Thekla, and Domentzia's Sabina were piled like puppies not far from her feet, along with two of the younger maids. Catella and Ariadne were dozing off a bit to her right, and she could hear Verina and Ismenia snoring lightly behind her in chairs brought for the older ladies.

Birdsong and a full stomach will do that, Brithwynn thought, *especially when they follow hard work.*

She smiled in the rosy afternoon sunlight and got a little more comfortable on the pillows. Viviana had the right idea.

* * *

"Look to the king!" a rough male voice shouted.

Brithwynn awoke to chaos. A woman was screaming nearby, and her view of the rest of the pavilion was blocked by her Varangians and a few other armed men who appeared to be members of the King's Guard.

She started to sit up, but suddenly Valgarðr and Eogan were there on top of her, pushing her down into the cushions.

Eogan rolled off of her immediately and sprang into a low crouch, from which he surveyed the pavilion and its environs.

"Down, Eiríni!" Valgarðr growled through bared teeth. "Stay down!"

"But what –"

"Don't ask, just listen!" Valgarðr growled again. "Stay down if you want to live."

Valgarðr's words chilled her to the bone. Even during their escape from Constantinopolis, when her enemies had been closest, he had never used that tone with her.

Then it struck her.

Valgarðr believed she was in more danger now than when she was surrounded by a palaceful of her enemies.

She couldn't breathe. Valgarðr's weight seemed multiplied, till it was greater than the weight of the heavens Atlas was said to bear upon his shoulders.

She opened her mouth, but she couldn't inhale enough to speak.

She could have been turned to stone, a victim of Medusa, save that her lungs burned with the need for air.

She –

"Let her up." Verina's cool voice swept over her like a zephyr. "She's terrified and cannot breathe."

"Not while the assassin –"

"He's far from here, if he still runs free. And you have Eirini well-surrounded," Verina rebuked him. "Now let her up before the poor girl suffocates!"

Valgarðr rose to a crouch, then looked around and exchanged looks with Eogan and a couple of her other men. They had formed a wall around her and the other ladies, who huddled low on the cushions, the rosy sunlight and birdsong forgotten.

Frustration and anger caught in Brithwynn like a fire.

"What is going on?" she demanded, rising to her elbows before a look at Valgarðr's face stopped her cold.

"The king is dead," Valgarðr replied. "We have to get you out of here."

"Dead!" She tried to sit up, only to see three different shields lock into place around her.

"*What happened?*" Brithwynn demanded.

"Someone," Verina breathed, sinking to her knees against Brithwynn's back and wrapping her arms around her, "sent an assassin to kill the king. The guard is now chasing him down, those who aren't here. So he'll be dead or captured by nightfall."

She looked around as well as she could, surrounded as they were with Varangians and King's Guards. Most of the other ladies were with her on the cushions, though another knot of guardsmen probably defended the queen and the king's body. The screaming seemed to come from there, though the sound had changed and was slowly quieting.

Beyond the pavilion, many people were running one direction or another, but as she watched they seemed to be gathering around the pavilion. A growing crowd of Meridians stood with their backs to the pavilion, armed with an assortment of weapons and handy tools.

Like her Varangians, few of the other guardsmen were fully armed; most wore only their everyday clothing. But Brithwynn had never been so glad that her wild Varangians were never less than fully armed.

Her father had employed hundreds of Varangians, but she'd never seen his guardsmen move so quickly to defend him. She'd certainly never seen so many regular people come to his defense. Rituals and processions were one thing, actual danger was quite another.

And there was still a risk of further attacks. The guardsmen's behavior made that clear.

"They're... they're sure he ran?"

"He came out of the woods to shoot the king," Valgarðr replied. "Trying to pass as a laborer, probably worked until a crossbow bolt came out of nowhere. Some of the Guard were after him before he got back to the treeline."

"And now... what?"

"Now?" Valgarðr looked around. "We guard here until we can get you back to the palace. Whenever *that* is."

Brithwynn tried to relax into Verina's maternal embrace, though she couldn't keep from looking from Valgarðr to Eogan to Hjorygg, Earnwulfe, and the others. The guardsmen scanned the treeline as if watching for an army or a single rabbit-sized assassin to emerge from its shadows, springing into existence in the moment of attack.

Her fellow ladies looked fearful or defiant. Or both.

Thekla looked ready to cry. Brithwynn tried to smile at her, but her smile felt more like a grimace. She looked over at Domentzia, who held her eating dagger as if she intended to use it against an attacker. And Juliana –

Juliana looked like she'd noticed something beyond the pavilion.

"Look sharp, men!" a guardsman shouted, far to her left. "The carriages approach!"

Brithwynn turned toward the guardsman, as if she expected to be able to see anything through the shields and the press of bodies that surrounded her. She couldn't, of course, but it looked like everyone else turned that way as well.

Everyone except Valgarðr and a few of the other guardsmen. *They* continued to scan the surroundings, watching for any sign of danger.

But nobody attacked, as three closed carriages rolled up and the guardsmen rushed them into one of the waiting carriages. Valgarðr helped Brithwynn to her feet and sent her off at a run, surrounded by Kormákr, Eogan, Ragnar, and Hjorygg, then turned to Verina.

"I should be glad you're not set to protect *me*," Verina grumbled at him as he helped her to her feet. "You'd break a hip or something before you even knew what you were doing."

"Not at all, Hypatissa," he replied. "They built you from stone, back when rocks were soft and you could make anything from them."

"Rocks chip."

Brithwynn was bundled into the first carriage before she had a moment to regret it.

For once, Brithwynn didn't mind. The closed carriage had almost the security of stone. She didn't even mind that the guard had kept pushing ladies into the royal carriage until no one else could be pushed in. Even the queen had a lady perched on her lap, and the floor was packed just as tight.

A semi-hysterical part of Brithwynn kept asking what would happen if the extra weight panicked the horses or if one of the axles broke. Would they cushion each other if the carriage flipped, or would they be thrown all the worse?

She kept her mouth firmly closed on those questions, though her lips trembled.

Thekla was crying, as were many of the others. Of all the ladies crammed into the carriage, only a few of the oldest ones seemed dry-eyed and relatively calm.

And she could feel her panic returning, riding after them faster than the horsemen she could hear riding alongside the carriage.

Only one thing could save her from her panic.

Knowledge.

Basilissa Epiphania and her ladies had been closer to the king when the assassin struck.

Perhaps, just perhaps, they knew something more than her people had.

"What happened up there?" she managed to ask through trembling lips.

"Someone tried to assassinate the king," said Hypatissa Olga, the queen's chief lady-in-waiting, who sat even now between her queen and the throng. "That's all I know."

Olga might not know who was behind the assassin, but she did.

It was Ióannés.

His man had gotten so close!

Brithwynn felt the terror rising in her throat.

"Do they know –"

She wanted to ask why Ióannés would send his men so far after her but stopped herself before she incriminated herself, even before she saw Verina shake her head infinitesimally.

She knew. What she didn't know was why he would kill anyone around her, when she was the only one there who could even hope to claim the throne.

"– why they killed him?" she ended feebly.

Basilissa Epiphania burst into deep, gut-wrenching sobs, while Olga gave her a look that would cut stone.

"The assassin did not *kill* Basilios Timofei," she said coldly. "He had a crossbow bolt though the left shoulder, but he was upright and walking on his own when I saw the guards hustle him into a carriage. It looked like they barely kept him from joining the hunt for the assassin, and no wonder. He's seen worse in battle a hundred times over."

"I didn't mean..." Brithwynn started to say, as the ladies around her smiled feebly at the good news.

"And as to *why* they do that," the older lady continued, her voice harsh with emotion. "Here's a hard lesson for you. When the great houses of the Empire feud among themselves, the lesser houses are the first to suffer. And the greater the house, the greater and more wide-spread the suffering."

Brithwynn swallowed tightly, trying to remind herself that Olga had no idea who she was talking to. Not because she was wrong, but because she was right.

Her family was the greatest of them all.

How much suffering had they been responsible for, generation after generation?

How much more would they be responsible for, before the Lord's return ended their rule here on Earth?

Could they ever do enough good to make up for it?

* * *

They reached the palace without suffering a broken axle and were bundled inside at a moderately more relaxed pace than they'd been bundled into the carriages.

The queen and her ladies rushed to the royal chambers, followed by Domentzia, whose white face and frightened demeanor made her look ready to faint. Brithwynn told herself she should follow and help – somehow – but everywhere she turned, she encountered knots of worried Meridians.

Before she could make her way across the crowded hall, King Timofei entered, rushed across the hall by a knot of his guardsmen. Brithwynn saw only a flash of a drawn, white face before they were gone.

She moved to follow, before the path the courtiers had opened up closed in the king's wake.

Big drops of blood, some smeared by his guardsmen's boots, marked Basilios Timofei's path.

Brithwynn sank to the floor, a prayer on her lips that the king's household included a surgeon capable of saving him.

Her family's close and unique bond with the Eternal Father had to be worth something.

When Brithwynn next opened her eyes, she found herself surrounded by her own people and the men and women from the palace, all in postures of prayer.

Let this be enough, Father, she thought. *Send your angels to defend this good king from the enmity of my brother Ióannés. Let them guide the hands of the household surgeon and the ladies who assist him.*

She tucked her chin against her folded hands and continued praying, as the low rumble of voices around her rose and fell in the prescribed chants as time fell into eternity and the king's surgeon battled for his life.

* * *

Lord of the Powers be with us, Brithwynn intoned along with everyone else in the hall, *for in times of distress we have no other help but you. Lord of the Powers, have mercy on –"*

"Alleluia!" someone near the front of the hall shouted out, joined by other voices throughout the packed space. "Alleluia! Alleluia!"

Brithwynn opened her eyes as the throne room erupted into cheers and shouts of exultation. She turned toward the door leading to the king's chamber and was... under-impressed.

Basilios Timofei *should* have been recovering in his bed, but such luxuries cost too much for kings and emperors to allow themselves. He walked slowly into the hall, a clean tunic and thick bandage helping to disguise his wound, if not his pallor. He sat carefully on his throne, then raised a hand to acknowledge the joyful shouting that filled the hall.

The whole time, Basilissa Epiphania kept her eyes on him, watching for any sign that his exertions were too much. She sat gingerly on her own throne, ready to move in an instant.

Brithwynn had been sitting in the greater audience chamber of the Blachernai with most of the royal family when her father had first started showing signs of the poisoning that eventually killed him. Ióannés had been conveniently far off in Cilicia, supposedly clearing out nests of pirates who were troubling Mediterranean shipping, while Isaak had been away quelling rebellious tribespeople in the mountains north of Dalmatia as he tried to build his own reputation. But Augousta

Maria had worn the same look when Papa's pallor and weakness became apparent.

Brithwynn believed in the reality of Epiphania' concern far more than she'd ever believed in Maria's. Though Maria had *probably* not had a hand in Ióannés' patricide, any concern she had at Papa's weakness was more likely due to the danger it put her and her sons in.

But the ways of government left no room for human weakness or concern, so Basilios Timofei had to present a strong façade while fighting for his life, just like Papa had.

She prayed Timofei would survive better than Papa had, though his waxen appearance didn't give her much cause for hope. And the need to reassure his people didn't help.

"My people!" he said, at something less than his normal volume. "As you see, I am well. The Lord Almighty sent his angels to turn the bow of the assassin sent against me this day."

The hall resounded with shouts of praise until Basilios Timofei raised his hand again.

"But dark days lie ahead of us, for the civil war between the pretenders to the holy throne of the blessed Augoustos Alexios has reached our quiet kingdom. One of them thought to better his position by forcing us to rally to his banners. And where one attacks, others will as well, to bring us to their side or deny our support to the first."

Basilios Timofei leaned back in his throne and breathed shallowly for several minutes, his face deadly pale.

If he was trying to convince his people that he was well, Brithwynn thought, *he'd be better off coming up with an excuse to return to his chamber.*

"But we will trust in the Lord Almighty and our own strong arms to defend our kingdom Meridia against the incursions of all pretenders to the Eternal Throne until God in his infinite wisdom places His chosen one upon it."

Please, Heavenly Father, Brithwynn breathed, *don't let it be Ióannés. A man who would murder his own* father — *not to mention several of our cousins and brothers — would be a poor representative of Your Holiness here on Earth and a dangerous occupant of the Eternal Throne.*

"His holy priests will now begin a week of prayer and fasting, asking the Lord's continued blessings upon us and His protection during this time of civil war. I beg all of you to share in this sacrament of prayer and thanksgiving."

He leaned back again, taking a long drink from the goblet Basilissa Epiphania passed him, of wine mixed only lightly with water.

Brithwynn realized she was holding her breath and let it out slowly. As she did so, she realized that she stood beside one of Domentzia's ladies, young Sabina, who had been picking apples with some of her girls just this morning.

She forced herself to smile tightly at the girl. Only then did she realize that she had been crying.

She reached out a hand, and Sabina clutched it the way a drowning man might.

Brithwynn felt far too much like a drowning man herself.

* * *

"The Guard have returned!" the young guardsman announced from the doorway. "With the attacker and... several wounded."

Two guardsmen half-carried a bloody captive between them, his arms bound tightly to an oak staff, but Brithwynn couldn't look away from the guardsmen being carried in behind them. From where she stood, she couldn't tell if they were alive or dead, lying as they were on improvised stretchers. Several other guardsmen walked with help or wore bloody bandages.

And some of them were hers.

Brithwynn realized with a start that she'd just assumed her men had all stayed with her after the attack and had since returned to the palace, though she hadn't actually noticed more than half of them in the chaos. But she saw Olav and Gothen among the returning warriors, and one of the heavily-bandaged men appeared to be Hrothgar.

She scanned the Meridian guardsmen for anyone else she recognized or any of their distinctive Varangian clothing and armor, but the Meridians' armor looked more like her Varangians' than she had realized.

Or perhaps it was just that they were both so different from the only other type of armor she'd ever seen, the elegant hammered lamellar of a Byzantine noble.

She squeezed through the crowded Meridians, trying to see which of the returning warriors numbered among her men. Several of her ladies followed her through the gaps she left, until Veronica was able to squeeze past her and lead the way. Ariadne and Thalassia followed, quick on her heels, and Brithwynn found it much easier to move through the crowd until she was close enough to see what was going on.

The apparent leader of the Meridian guardsmen knelt before his king, a reddening bandage on his left arm where one of the enemy's swords had bitten him above his shield. Behind him, two other warriors stood over the captive, now pressed to the floor. The rest of the guardsmen stood behind them, arrayed in a semicircular space that the Meridian courtiers had opened up for them.

Now that she had a better view of the men, she recognized Thorfinn and Ranvalðr among them. Both were wounded, though only Ranvalðr's leg wound appeared serious.

"The assassin was not alone?" Basilios Timofei asked as she drew near enough to hear them, his voice quietly cold. "I know one man did not outfight so many of you."

"No, Basilios," the guardsman admitted. "The wretch led us straight into a trap."

"If I had any doubts that this is because I rebuffed the prince's emissary," Basilios Timofei said, his voice dark with cold anger, "they would be gone now. How did it happen?"

"We chased him into the deep woods overlooking the Tylihul," the guardsman continued. "They were on us before we knew they were there, firing and running down the hill at us."

"And our men with only what they'd taken for a *peaceful* outing," Veronica whispered in sorrowful admiration.

"No wonder so many of them got hurt or –"

Thalassia clapped her hands over her mouth.

"– outnumbered us two to one, Basilios," the guardsman was saying.

"They pressed us to the edge of the precipice before one of the Trimarians took out their leader and we were able to get them on the run."

"Who is this hero?" Basilios Timofei asked, looking toward the gathered soldiers.

"His name was Brendan," the guardsman replied. "He and the enemy leader fought back and forth at the edge of the precipice, till he gutted his enemy with his spear. But they were too close to the edge, and the man took him over before we could stop him."

Brithwynn's heart plummeted.

Brendan was *dead*?

He'd always been wild, even for one of her Varangians. Even – or especially – in battle, his eyes always twinkled with mischief. Brithwynn had known him since he served in her father's honor guard, before Papa gave her her own guard and assigned him and Valgarðr to it. He could always be counted on to jump into trouble feet-first, whether it was infighting among the palace soldiers or romantic entanglements with one of the maids.

But what stood out the most about him to her was that he always seemed to be laughing, at least with his eyes, no matter what was going on. Even when he was being taken to task for his latest escapades.

Once, when she was ten, she'd asked him to explain why he laughed so much.

"The gods meant for us to laugh," he'd told her. "Look at the world they put us in and tell me it's not so!"

That had been shortly after she'd realized that the Augousta Maria was scheming to place one of her own sons on the Eternal Throne, in place of the obvious heir Ióannés, whom she'd still adored. The knowledge had weighed heavily upon her, and she'd been offended by his reply until she realized that his Hibernian gods were strange enough to be amused by such things.

Verina had thought he was an incredibly bad influence and done her best to keep him away from Brithwynn and the girls, though she'd still seen her laughing at his jokes from time to time.

And now he was dead.

"Varus did worse with better odds," Basilios Timofei was telling the guardsman when Brithwynn forced her attention back to the present. "You caught this worm and brought me back my legions."

"Thanks to Spatharios Brendan," he replied, kneeling even lower. "We owe our lives to him."

"His lady will wish to hear this from you," Basilios Timofei said, motioning her toward the dais. The Meridian warrior stood and stepped back, bowing his head respectfully.

Brithwynn stepped forward uncertainly as the handful of Meridians ahead of her drew aside. She stopped a little less than an orguiá away from the king and nodded solemnly at him, still numb from the news of Brendan's death and uncertain what to do.

"Kyria Eiríni," Basilios Timofei said, after coughing and clearing his voice to speak more loudly. "You have only been here a few days, and yet you and yours have had quite an impact on Our court."

More than you know, Basilios, Brithwynn thought. *More than you know.*

"And now your staunch guardsman Brendan gave his life to aid my men in bringing an assassin to justice," he added, aiming a disparaging look at the captive his men still stood over.

"Spatharios Brendan saved our lives," the leader of the guardsmen said, bowing his head and bringing his hand to his heart. "And your other men fought beside us as equals, though they had sworn no oaths to us. That makes them my brothers."

"I cannot replace your guardsman," Basilios Timofei added, "but I would pay you the wergelðr due you for his service. Dmitry!"

An older man stepped forward while Brithwynn was trying to understand what he meant. He nodded curtly at her and placed a small bag of coins in her hand.

Gold for a life, she thought. *Or silver, I suppose.*

Such a cold exchange.

"I would give my own gift for his memory," the guardsman added. He withdrew a short, curved dagger from his belt, kneeling before her as he presented it. "May it serve you as well as he did."

Brithwynn quickly slipped the bag to Ariadne and reached for the dagger the rough guardsman offered her. It suited him, suited Brendan still more.

She caught her breath, but not before she'd burst into tears.

* * *

Brithwynn stood where she'd retreated after her interview with the king, watching as he and his men questioned the would-be assassin.

It was brutal, but she needed to know if the assassin gave his master's name. She needed to know if it was Ióannés.

But who else could it be, really?

Basilissa Epiphania had watched intently when the questioning started, but she had blanched and averted her eyes when the guardsmen who held the assassin ripped his kamision from him and started beating him, filling the hall with the hollow sounds of staves striking broken flesh. His moans and cries made Brithwynn feel sick, even as she tried to remind herself that men like him could only be broken in such a manner.

But she couldn't help herself. She turned away in revulsion when a particularly well-delivered blow sent the man's cries into the falsetto range.

When she turned back, Basilissa Epiphania had turned whiter than Basilios Timofei. She had her hands raised and was speaking quietly with him.

He held up his right hand and commanded the guardsmen to stop, then stood, swaying. Basilissa Epiphania took his arm and spoke quietly to him.

He shook his head, slowly, carefully.

They walked slowly out of the hall. Behind them, the guardsmen half-carried, half-dragged their captive.

Most of the courtiers quickly returned to their prayers or quotidian activities after the king and queen left, but Brithwynn felt like a boat that had been raised far up the beach by the rising tide, only to be abandoned there when the tide retreated.

She *should* go watch the questioning, to learn whatever she could from Ióannés' man. But the thought made her sick.

Not just because of the way he was being questioned. That was to be expected, given the low sort of creature he was. But sooner or later he would break and tell his questioners everything he knew about Ióannés.

Or he would protect his secret until his body gave out, and they would never learn what she needed to know.

She didn't know which one she feared more.

That uncertainty kept her rooted in place, like a weak-willed courtier.

Papa would have reminded her that she was born to be more than that. A ruler, he would say, must always be in control of what happens in his realm, even – or especially – when it was difficult.

But she was not in control.

She jumped when a hand suddenly touched hers.

It was young Domentzia, her face white and streaked from crying.

"Eiríni, can you come with me?" Domentzia said quietly. "Mother wants to speak with you."

Brithwynn felt her face lose its color. Had they been able to make the assassin speak after all? Had they discovered her relationship to his master?

"I'm sure it's nothing," Domentzia said, misreading her fear. "Father is well and just needed some rest."

It's never nothing, Brithwynn thought. *Even if they don't know it was Ióannés, it's never nothing when the lives of kings are at stake.*

Brithwynn followed Domentzia out of the hall and upstairs to the bedrooms. She half-expected them to go to the queen's own chamber, but instead Domentzia led her to her own.

Basilissa Epiphania had doubted her story and come here to search for evidence. And she had found something. She must have, to want to see her at a time like this.

Given the assassination attempt on her husband, it was all too likely that she would think Brithwynn had been the assassin's master instead of his actual target.

But Basilissa Epiphania was alone in the room and stood by the room's small window, looking out at the fading daylight.

Brithwynn and Domentzia stood in the doorway a few moments before Basilissa Epiphania seemed to notice them. She turned and gestured for Domentzia to leave, waiting until the door was shut to speak.

"Kyria Eiríni," she said. "I must ask that you leave this house immediately!"

The queen was *asking* her to leave instead of telling her to leave, or ordering her guards in to take her into custody?

"Go, child!" Basilios Epiphania continued. "Leave tonight, if you can, or tomorrow at first light!"

It wasn't that the queen had found something that told her who she really was.

She seemed almost afraid for Brithwynn, as if –

"Is the king –" she gulped, unable to say "dead." She sat down hard on the edge of the bed, glad it was there.

"No, praise Heaven," the queen replied, crossing herself quickly. "But this is not the end, damn this war!"

This war that her brother had started.

"Be glad you're not from a major house of the Empire, my dear. Yours might even be small enough to survive. But those of us with any position in society? This war will kill us all before it's done!"

Brithwynn could only imagine what Basilissa Epiphania would think if she only knew Brithwynn had *brought* this war to their doorstep. She'd be glad that Ióannés' men would surely catch up with her the moment she left the relative security of Ióannésopolis.

The queen would think she deserved to die, for having brought the war into her kingdom and her home.

"I've half a mind to send Domentzia with you into exile, get her away from all this before they try again," Basilissa Epiphania continued, oblivious to the emotions that must surely be playing across her face.

"But..."

How to tell her that the attack on Basilios Timofei must surely have been brought on by her presence, that Prinkepissa Domentzia would surely die along with her when Ióannés' assassins caught up with her?

"No, you're right," Basilissa Epiphania agreed, looking hard at Brithwynn's tear-streaked face. "Your honor guard alone is almost too big to escape attention, and it would take a far larger one to keep you both safe if you were discovered."

She grimaced. "One so big it would announce to the world that they escorted a valuable target."

Basilissa Epiphania rose and paced back to the window, her entire body taut with nervous energy.

"What will you do?" Brithwynn managed to ask.

The queen was silent for several minutes, looking out over the city as if trying to spot the dangers that threatened her family, then spoke without turning around.

"You've given me an idea," she said, almost to herself. "Your story, it just seems too perfectly timed. You *happened* to be in Ansteoria visiting family when the emperor was murdered? *Coincidentally*, you decided to come home to Trimaria right then?"

Brithwynn's blood ran cold.

"No," she said, either in answer to Brithwynn's choked reply or to her own questions. "You can keep your secret, I won't ask who you really are. Maybe you're Ansteorian, maybe you're from one of the central provinces. It doesn't matter. But news of the Emperor's assassination reached your family before it spread to us out on the borders, and your father sent you into exile to save your life. Maybe you really have family in Trimaria, maybe they're just your father's partisans. Maybe they're sending you even further from the center of this maelstrom!" she added, her voice rising hysterically. "But you're not the only heir who can be sent away to safety!"

The queen had come far too close to the truth, but she still didn't seem to blame her for it.

Brithwynn couldn't trust her voice. As it was, she felt like she had when she'd awakened to learn of the assassin. A heavy weight of boiling acid sat in the pit of her stomach, waiting to tip over and eat her alive.

She stood, amazed to feel her legs shake. She ran her hands down her thighs and walked over to the queen, willing her legs to be steady.

Basilissa Epiphania looked over and held out her hands, then pressed Brithwynn to her.

"Don't cry, my dear," she said. "This is the way of the world, and you'll learn to survive in it. We all do, even though there are few enough people you can trust in it. But for your youth and because you gave me the idea that may save my daughter, I swear to Our Holy Lord in Heaven that I'll not breath a word of this to anyone. Even Timofei."

She held Brithwynn out at arm's length and looked her in the eye, her gaze neither offering nor allowing any dissembling.

"Just do me one small favor, 'Kyria' Eiríni. If you ever see us again in this world, look kindly on us. I know we're backwoods royals from the outskirts of the Empire, and you would probably not even give us the time of day if you were back at home in your palace.

"I'm not judging you, child," she added, misunderstanding the shock on Brithwynn's face. "All the powerful families of the central provinces look down on us out here. But think well of us, and look out for Domentzia if you ever can."

"I will, Basilissa," Brithwynn replied, her voice trembling. "I hope I have that opportunity someday."

She kissed the queen's hands and turned away before bursting into tears.

* * *

Verina and Ismenia must have been waiting just outside the door to her chamber, because they had their arms around her almost as soon as Brithwynn realized that Basilissa Epiphania had left the room.

She got her tears back under control as well as she could and asked them the question that had been burning in her mind since she first woke up under the pavilion.

"Did we bring this on them?" she whispered.

"Hush, child!" Verina admonished her. "How can you think that?

Are you responsible for the wind and waves? The flooding that took Prinkeps Stephanos?"

As Brithwynn shook her head, she continued.

"Then how can you think this is your fault?"

"But if... if an assassin..."

"If *anyone*," Brithwynn heard the circuitous reference to Ióannés, "had sent an assassin after you and had known you were there, the assassin would have gone after *you*, not the king."

"But..."

"We were all asleep, but the king was awake," Ismenia put in, "And even though Basilios Timofei was surely enjoying some cider with his men, you were still a much easier target than he was."

"The assassin would never have gone after the more difficult target if you were who he was really after," Verina concluded.

"So the assassin was really after Basilios Timofei after all?" Brithwynn asked, feeling foolish.

"You're not the only person Sebastokrator Ióannés – or any of the other would-be emperors – has reason to want dead," Verina said, her voice calm and tender.

"Just the one we care about," Ismenia winked at her.

"Think about when you play zatrikion," Verina added. "You don't just try to capture the king, you also try to take all your opponent's other pieces, even the lowest soldiers. If you take enough, you don't even need to take his king, because he's powerless to take yours."

"They're playing a massive game of zatrikion across the entire empire," Verina explained. "Every provincial king, every major noble – and some of the minor ones – is a soldier in somebody's zatrikion army, one that must be taken or killed if you want to beat them. And the players you're sharing a board with are truly playing the game of kings. It's win or die for them, and I can assure you that none of them are ready to die. Ióannés isn't the only one who's a threat to you, just the biggest threat."

"So we didn't bring this on them?" Brithwynn asked.

"I tell you you're fighting in the bloodiest game of zatrikion ever played, and you ask about the soldiers." Verina shook her head, smiling. "But no, we didn't bring this on them. We're just trying to survive it."

* * *

"You're leaving tonight?" Timofei winced as he sat up, though he was quick to hide it. "Isn't it almost sundown?"

"Yes, Basilios," Brithwynn replied. "My people tell me that's for the best."

"Good," he replied. "They're right, of course. We wouldn't want you getting caught up in all this."

If he only knew! Brithwynn thought. *He would surely turn her over to her enemies, if only to save is family and his kingdom. He wouldn't have a choice.*

"I have failed you as a host, Kyria Eiríni," Basilios Timofei added, "but I may be able to make up for my failure. I can give you enough arms and armor so you and your ladies can ride as Varangian warriors until you're out of danger."

"You would do this for me?" Brithwynn asked, surprised.

"The Lord Above tells us that the protection of one's guests is among the most sacred of any lord's duties, most particularly when he is king of his own lands."

"Thank you, Basilios," Brithwynn replied, humbled that this noble king would think first of her safety when his own was so clearly endangered.

"Think nothing of it, child," Basilios Timofei replied. "I'd send a detachment of my men to guard you to the border, but it seems I need my men here." He grimaced. "And the extra men may even increase your danger, if anyone is watching."

As Ióannés' men certainly were.

"Because they'd bring extra attention."

"True," he nodded. "You're a smart girl, Kyria. You see my quandary."

"My own men will be enough, I'm sure," Brithwynn said, hoping that she spoke the truth.

"Ride swiftly," Basilios Timofei continued. "I know you probably spend less time ahorse than girls your age did in your mother's or grandmother's generation, but now's no time for slow riding and frequent stops."

He paused for breath, then muttered, "Constantinopolis has us turning our women into nuns and our men into priests. Their priests claim it's God's will, but –"

He pursed his lips and blew explosively, then grimaced. "That may be fine in the heart of the Empire, but behavior like that will get us to Heaven's grace a little sooner than we'd like, out here."

That was because Constantinopolis was Heaven, Brithwynn thought. Or at least as close to it as mere mortals could build, even with the Heavenly Father's blessing and guidance.

Which sometimes left a lot to be desired.

Basilios Timofei took another careful breath and looked at her, his mien solemn.

"Don't ride like a nun out here unless you wish to become a dead nun."

Brithwynn hoped she'd had enough practice riding by now that she wouldn't get herself and her people killed.

"Your man Valgarðr seems to know what he's about," Basilios Timofei continued after a moment. "But if I can make a suggestion, you'll make the best time on the King's Road, better than on the Great Coastal Road or the Kryvyi Way. It's well-maintained even through the marshes, so your men will have solid ground if they need to fight."

Some part of her had known all along that it would be necessary for her men to fight in her defense if they were ever discovered. But now, with several of her men freshly wounded in battle against Ióannés' men, the thought of battle seemed terrifyingly real.

But would it be wise to take his recommendation?

She didn't believe that Basilios Timofei would intentionally set her up to be assassinated. Not really, not so long as her secret was safe. But if he wasn't the only one who knew which route he'd suggested? Or that he'd suggested the road that sounded like the obvious choice?

Of course, Brithwynn thought, *even here the walls may have ears, though any who spied on his own king was nothing but a traitor.*

Unless he was worse than that, one of Ióannés' own men. Then he, or his fellows, would see her dead, and all in service to his liege.

* * *

The old quilted kamision would have fit Ióannés or Isaak better than it fit her, but the excess bulk helped to disguise her slender feminine build. With the simple lorica and helmet Basilios Timofei's quartermaster had given her, Brithwynn didn't even recognize herself in the burnished bronze mirror.

"Are you ready for this?" Verina asked. "If anyone's after you, this could get... interesting."

"When hasn't it been?" Brithwynn asked, turning around.

She laughed. Maybe a *little* hysterically.

Verina wore an old centurion's breastplate and helmet. A pair of striped Varangian breeches covered her legs between her quilted kamision and an old pair of greaves.

She looked like she could be Valgarðr's commander.

Incongruously, she also wore a huge grin that made her look at least twenty years younger.

"You look like a soldier!" Brithwynn exclaimed.

"I *was* a soldier," Verina smiled. "I was a young woman when I came to Constantinopolis with your mother."

"You – ohh!" Brithwynn exclaimed, as Verina's grin stretched even wider.

"But I thought... you couldn't ride," she added, perplexed.

"I could," Verina replied. "I just got old and rusty. Too many decades' worth of rusty."

She laughed. "Like this armor."

"You don't look it," Brithwynn said.

"I am," Verina said. "Though I've surely maligned this armor. It may be old, but it's been well tended."

6

The Night Road

The moon was just rising over the eastern hills when Valgarðr led them out the city's south entrance toward the King's Road. To their right, the sun had closed to little more than a hand's breadth above the horizon.

No one had complained at their precipitous departure, though many of the women had blanched when they saw how badly wounded several of the men were. Rafn was still only functional while ahorse – and in bed, if what she heard from his blushing young bride was half true. Now Ranvalðr and Hrothgar joined him on the disabled list; Hrothgar should have been put to bed.

Brithwynn hoped he would have a chance to recover.

Of course, if he didn't, it would probably be because they had been attacked and were all dead.

A part of her wanted to put heels to Iphigenia's flanks and speed through the darkening countryside, to escape the dangers they'd encountered in Ióannésopolis and to experience the heady rush of freedom that already seemed to be fading.

But too much haste would draw the attention of Ióannés' spies, and it could even bring its own dangers as the sunlight faded.

So she held herself to the pace Valgarðr set, as daylight faded and a new day began.

* * *

"Are we riding all night?" Thekla asked, her voice quivering. "Won't the wolves get us?"

"Better the wolves who fight with teeth and claw than the ones who use blade and bow," Ismenia told her, quoting a proverb that Brithwynn suddenly realized belonged far more to this wild countryside than to the marble halls where she had first heard it.

Though it was even more true when the wolves in question preferred to kill with poisons and lies.

She shuddered, though nobody seemed to notice in the moonlight.

"Wolves don't attack large parties like ours," Kormákr told the girl from his position at the edge of the unit.

"Now, if we stopped, that would be a different story!" Nikifor laughed. "Grrrow!"

"Stop it!" Theadora demanded.

"It's true!" he retorted. "You'd need a mucking big fire to keep them away, and even then you'd better watch the shadows for their glowing eyes!"

"I said *stop it*," the lady growled, gesturing at Thekla. "Don't you think the poor child has been frightened enough today?"

"Don't you worry, child," Hjorvgg said. "We won't let either kind of wolf have you."

"You are *such* a wolf!" Earnwulfe laughed from the other side of the road.

"I thought I was a goat?"

"You are! One wicked old goat!"

"Only another old goat would know!"

Hjorvgg made a strange noise in reply that Brithwynn assumed must be the sound a goat made. Or at least his interpretation of it.

Several of the men laughed.

"You sound like you're getting... gelded," Kormákr said, substituting the polite word for whatever he would have said if she and her ladies hadn't been present.

"Memories from when you were a kid?" Thorfinn jeered.

"At least they didn't make me eat mine!"

"Only because they couldn't *find* them!"

"Quiet, you imbeciles!" Valgardr hissed. "Were you raised in a barn?"

The cacophony of animal noises he got in reply seemed answer enough.

* * *

"I don't like this," Valgarðr told her quietly, his eyes never stopping as he scanned the trees that bordered the King's Road, overshadowing the tightly-fitted stone cobbles and limiting the moonlight that reached them, just as the moon sank toward the horizon.

Within minutes, they would be riding in the dark.

"Can we make camp?"

"Not unless you want to see what manner of wolves follow us," he replied.

It wasn't like any of this looked like a place where they could camp, Brithwynn thought. *Though she was almost tired enough to sleep in her saddle.*

No. She'd caught herself dozing off more than once. She was tired enough to sleep in her saddle, except that she probably couldn't stay in it.

And now something had Valgarðr spooked. It kept getting better and better.

But her mother had surely experienced worse on campaign. As had Valgarðr, Verina, and probably any of her other people who had ever seen battle.

She inhaled deeply of the cool night air and tried to force herself awake.

"What do you recommend?" she asked.

"The land's too flat and soft around here to offer a good defensive position," he said, thinking. "We could attempt one anyway, but it would be a losing proposition against anything resembling similar numbers. And they won't attack without a serious advantage."

Would it be too much to hope that meant they wouldn't attack?

"Worse, a third of the forces I *appear* to have are women who've never fought or who haven't fought in years," Valgarðr continued. "And a third of my remaining forces are wounded, so anyone who attacks us will outnumber us worse than they know."

"That's what you *don't* recommend doing," Brithwynn said, trying not to snap at him. "What *do* you recommend doing?"

Valgarðr blew out forcefully through his mouth and noise.

"We ride, Eirini," he said. "At a good, solid canter, not a gallop. That – and our numbers – might be enough to scare off any brigands, though I wouldn't lay odds it'll stop anyone else. We hit any sign of trouble, you and yours ride at the fastest gallop you can manage, like your lives depend on it. My fastest men will stick with you while the rest of us hold them off to give you time to escape."

"And how do we meet back up afterwards?" Brithwynn asked, though she had a sinking feeling that she knew the answer already.

"Those of us who survive the encounter will find you," Valgarðr replied, his tone brooking no refusal.

She had thought she understood that some, possibly even all, of her people might die if they were attacked. But the fact that Valgarðr expected fatalities made it more real, more terrifying.

Not for the first time, she prayed for an uneventful ride.

It only took Valgarðr moments to tell his men the plan, a little longer for him and Verina to get the women and Niphon to understand what they were supposed to do.

Brithwynn could almost understand why many of her older ladies, who had fought alongside her mother as young women, would choose to fight instead of run. But Niphon – of all people – had insisted he would stand and fight with the other men.

Stick a scribe in armor, and he'd think he was some kind of Varangian.

* * *

An arrow whizzed through the night, striking a tree just as Verina passed it.

Brithwynn caught her breath and realized she'd stopped, just as Verina grabbed her reins and took off down the road at a faster pace than Brithwynn had ever ridden before.

They had splashed through a shallow ford and gotten back on the road to race nearly to the top of the next gentle rise a hundred or so orguiáe further on before Verina slowed, allowing Brithwynn to look around to see who had reached this point of relative safety with them.

Ariadne and Thalassia rode close beside her on her right, with Helena a little further behind. On the other side of Verina, she thought she saw Penelope and Viviana.

"Are we stopping here?" Aglaia asked from beyond Theadora as Verina turned her horse back toward the battle they had escaped. Now that they were stopped, she saw that Catella, Basina and Thekla had also made it.

That was all of them, except for Veronica and Zephrina, who had argued that they should be able to stay and fight.

Even the maids had made it this far, though they kept themselves a little apart from the ladies and were now looking back the way they had come with varying degrees of trepidation.

Just like most of the ladies.

Once she realized where they were, Brithwynn suspected Zephrina and Veronica weren't feeling trepidation. They had stopped just on this side of the ford and were already guarding their backtrail with the seven guardsmen who had ridden with them this far, watching for any signs that the battle was coming their way.

Brithwynn had heard that Zephrina's mother had taught her more of fighting than the nobles of Constantinopolis had thought appropriate for a girl. Now she hoped that the lady had been her own mother's equal and a better teacher.

"For now," Verina replied through gritted teeth, her attention on the road and the distant sounds of battle. "Be ready to ride if they approach."

"What do we do if we have to fight?" Ariadne asked a few moments later, her voice tight and highly controlled. "Most of us don't know how."

It can't be that hard, Brithwynn told herself. *If Mother could do it, I could surely learn. With time and a good teacher, anyway.*

One of which I don't have.

"We fight as a last resort, ladies," Verina commanded. "Better to ride and make them chase us than to stand and let them overwhelm us."

Brithwynn glanced over at Verina, hoping that wasn't all the advice she had.

Evidently she wasn't the only one, or Verina knew that Brithwynn and the other young ladies needed more than that.

"Keep riding forward till the enemy give you no other choice, then push past them and keep going as soon as you can," Verina added. "Keep your shield up, it's the only thing standing between you and those who want to kill you. Keep together. And keep your eyes open."

"What about our swords?" Viviana asked.

"If they make you stop and fight," Verina replied, "hit them with your sword as hard and as often as you can, until they aren't in your way anymore."

* * *

The riders down at the ford seemed to grow restive as the noises of battle carried through the still night air, silencing their horse's whinnies as they stared out at the night-darkened forest.

Were they as torn as she was, wanting to know how her people were doing but afraid, half ready to fly through the night to some distant refuge?

Or were they instead torn between their duty to guard her and their desire to ride to their companions' aid?

The sick fear in the pit of her stomach made Brithwynn feel unworthy. Mother had fought, had earned a reputation as a warrior and a leader of warriors. She *should* have inherited that warrior's iron stomach, but instead she wanted to flee like some cowardly child.

"Calm, Eirini," Verina said, her voice pitched low so it wouldn't carry. "The worst part of a battle is always the waiting, when the time for strategy is over and the time for tactics not yet arrived. Especially when your companions already fight."

Brithwynn tried to make herself calm down, but little she did seemed to have any effect.

Instead, she watched the riders at the ford as well as she could in the dark, saw when one horse and then another flicked their ears and whinnied in response to some noise she couldn't sort out from the more distant sounds of battle.

She was still ready to set her heels in Iphigenia's flanks and set off like the wind when a dark shape appeared over the hill on the other side of the river, but something held her back a moment.

In that moment, Zephrina spoke.

"It's Ismenia," she said. "And someone else."

"Watch the rise," Verina whispered harshly to her. "And flee if you see *anyone* else."

* * *

Niphon lay across his saddle on the second horse, barely moving as Ismenia guided their horses through the dark up the hill to the rest of the ladies.

"The boy took an arrow," she said as she drew close enough to be heard. "It's not bad, but he fainted at the sight."

Theadora rode up to Niphon and examined his arm under the uncertain light of the little torch Thalassia had re-lit as soon as they stopped. An arrow had passed under the layered strips of leather that protected his left shoulder and bit deeply into his flesh, pushing aside the leather strips on the back of his shoulder.

"I need a scarf or something to stop the bleeding," Theadora said, looking around. "And someone stronger than me to get this thing out."

Catella pulled something out of her saddlebags and rode up on

Niphon's other side, but Verina caught Brithwynn's attention when she pulled Ismenia aside.

Brithwynn followed, certain she was supposed to know whatever Ismenia had to say.

"How goes the battle?" Verina asked.

"They're no simple brigands," Ismenia replied, looking from Brithwynn to Verina. "Leaderless, but well trained. Our warriors may be better and Valgarðr's a good commander, but... It'll be a tough fight."

With that, she turned her horse around with a quick motion and rode back down the hill toward the ford and the fighting, disappearing into the night air before she was halfway down the hill.

Glossary

Some of these terms have multiple meanings. Rather than present you with the whole dictionary definition of a term, I've included just the one that's appropriate to the Saga.

Also, I'm sure everyone knows by now that the official name that historians use for the eastern half of the Roman Empire is "the Eastern Roman Empire." However, that's quite a mouthful and is no more appropriate to this saga than "Byzantine" is. In fact, you could argue that "Byzantine" is more appropriate, considering both the people of Constantinopolis and the wild northern Rús might at least recognize the term as a cognate of their city's former name or their name for the empire far to their south. So I'll use "Byzantine Empire" or simply "the Empire" here in the glossary, to be more approachable. In the Saga itself, I'll use "Basileia tôn Rhōmaiōn" or "Rhōmania," to be more immersive.

Aegis Rhōmaiōn: the term used in the Byzantine Empire for the protection offered by the Empire and the region receiving this protection and influence. This region included areas that weren't necessarily within the borders of the Empire but were virtually a part of it. In a modern sense, they were in a corresponding position to that of American overseas territories under the American Aegis.

Ansteoria: a fictional minor kingdom in the Aegis Rhōmaiōn, on the outskirts of the Empire. It corresponds to the portion of the Empire between the Danube and Dniester rivers.

Ásgarðr: the settlement Baldar established on the shores of Lake Ladoga once he became a successful trader. He named it for that other

Ásgarðr, because it seemed too perfect to be anything less than an echo of Ásgarðr on Midgarðr (Earth).

Augousta: the feminine form of Augoustos, which is more familiar in its Latin form of Augustus. Augousta was the title used for Byzantine empresses.

Augoustos: the Greek form of the Latin title Augustus. Augoustos was the title used for Byzantine emperors.

Autokratera: an alternative Byzantine term for Augousta, meaning "Empress."

Basileia tôn Rhōmaiōn: the Byzantine Empire's name for itself, a Greek translation of the Roman Empire's Latin name.

Basilios: the king of a satellite kingdom under the Aegis Rhōmaiōn.

Basilissa: the queen of a satellite kingdom under the Aegis Rhōmaiōn.

Blachernai Palace: the "new" palace in Constantinopolis, used by the Augoustos (Emperor) and his family. It was built in the eleventh century, when the Great Palace at the tip of the peninsula of Constantinopolis was seven centuries old and badly in need of restoration. The Blachernai Palace was built outside the Constantinian Wall but inside the Theodosian Wall.

Bysantinsk: the term used by Scandianavians and Rús for the Byzantine Empire. By the twelfth century, the Empire had expanded and contracted several times, though this book is set in a world where the Empire's borders remained at approximately its greatest extent, including the territories around the Black Sea and the eastern Mediterranean as far west as Italia.

Campus Martius: literally the "field of Mars," the Campus Martius in Constantinopolis and any other city in the Roman or Byzantine Empire was the place where soldiers assembled, trained, marched off to battle, and were released to return home.

Chrysókeras: The Golden Horn, the estuary and deep natural harbor that formed the northeastern boundary of the peninsula on which Constantinopolis was built.

Constantinopolis: the capital of the Byzantine Empire. The city was founded as Byzantion in the 650s or 660s BC (sources differ), during the reign of Byzas of Megara. It became part of the Roman Empire in 196 AD and was known as Byzantium until Constantine the Great moved the capital of the Empire there in 330 AD and renamed it.

Cubit: a unit of measure in use from ancient times, still in use in the Empire during the twelfth century. It was based on the length of a man's forearm and typically measured 44 cm or 18 inches.

Dalmatikion: a simple woolen gown, worn in the Empire by average citizens.

Dróttning: the Swedish word for queen.

Einherjar: a Scandinavian warrior's war band, this term is more famously associated with the warriors who fall in battle and await Ragnarök as part of Odin's great war band in Valhalla.

Eis Pegas: a minor gate in the sea walls of Constantinopolis

Eternal City: a Byzantine appellation for Constantinopolis.

Eternal Throne: a Byzantine appellation for the throne of the Byzantine Empire.

Fensalir: in Scandinavian mythology, the goddess Frigg's heaven, the great feasting-hall where she welcomes loving couples after their deaths.

Gardariki: the name in Norse sagas for the territory (considered to be either a principality or a kingdom) that Novgorod was capital of. It grew to become Russia.

Glenabenia: a fictional minor kingdom in the Aegis Rhōmaiōn, on the outskirts of the Empire. It corresponds to the portion of the Empire between the Dniester and Bug rivers.

Grœnlend: The medieval Scandinavian name for Greenland.

Gunnbjorn Skerries: a group of small islands between Iceland and Greenland, where a Scandinavian colony existed from circa 970 AD to the mid-fifteenth century.

Hertogi: a Norse noble title that meant "war-leader" and is thought to have been equivalent to duke.

Hertogakona: the feminine form of hertogi, a Norse noble title meaning "duchess."

Holmgarðr: the name for Novgorod used in the Norse sagas, originally just the stronghold 2 kilometers south of today's city center

Hypatissa: a Byzantine noble title equivalent to "baroness."

Írlend: the Scandinavian term for Ireland.

Jōl: Yule, the Scandinavian winter festival.

Kamision: a linen undergown or chemise, worn in the Empire by average citizens.

Knyaz: Rús for "king" or "prince."

Kyria: a Byzantine noble title equivalent to "lady."

Kyriatate: a Byzantine noble title higher than "lady" but lower than any of the other titles of nobility.

Meridia: a fictional minor kingdom in the Aegis Rhōmaiōn, on the outskirts of the Empire. It corresponds to the portion of the Empire between the Bug and Dnieper rivers.

Midgarðr: the term for Earth in Scandinavian mythology, it means "Middle Earth" and is one of the nine worlds believed to have been connected by the World Tree, Yggdrasil.

Mikligarðr: the medieval Scandinavian name for the city of Constanti-nopolis. The name meant "Great City."

Niðingr: a nothing, an honorless person, a scoundrel; someone who has earned his erasure from the community.

Nornir: the three Norns of Scandinavian mythology, the goddesses who shape the fates of mankind and of the gods.

Orguiá(e): a Classical and Byzantine Greek unit of measure, approx-imately equal to a person's two outstretched arms. That made it approximately six feet long, or just under two meters in length. The plural of *orguiá* is *orguiáe*.

Palla: a Roman and Byzantine wrap or scarf, essentially a cross between a rectangular veil and a light mantle. Women wore pallas over their heads and wrapped loosely around their bodies. They used large brooches to hold their pallas in place if they could afford to.

Porphyrogénita: a princess born to the reigning emperor. Like her siblings born after their father became emperor, her birth in a special room of the palace called the *porphyry* would be public proof of her legitimacy.

Porphyrogénnēti: all those legitimate children born to the reigning emperor. They would be born in a square room of the palace called the *porphyry*, where the floor and walls were covered in a rare purple marble. These children were literally "born to the purple."

Rhōmania: the Byzantine Empire's short name for itself, which translates to "Rome." The long form of their name for their empire is Basileia tôn Rhōmaiōn.

Rús: those Scandinavian explorers, mainly Swedish, who came to explore, settle, and trade along the riverways of what is now northwestern Russia.

Sebastokratissa: a female recognized heir to the Eternal Throne of the Byzantine Empire, or the wife of the Sebastokrator. This meant she was the Crown Princess of the Byzantine Empire.

Sebastokrator: the recognized heir to the Eternal Throne of the Basileia tôn Rhōmaiōn, the Crown Prince of the Byzantine Empire.

Serklend: the early medieval Scandinavian term for the "land of the Serkir," which is now usually thought to mean the land of the Saracens. This was presumably the Umayyad Caliphate (661-750 AD) or the earlier period of the Abbasid Caliphate (750-1258 AD). One theory explaining the meaning of the term "serkir" is that it means "shirt-wearers," as the long clothes of the Saracens resemble the loose linen serks that served as undershirts or chemises in Scandinavian dress at the time.

Skald: a medieval or Viking-age Scandinavian poet, who told stories in grand poetic form.

Spatharios: a noble title denoting knighthood, like "Sir."

Tagma: a large Byzantine military unit, which might be of battalion or regiment size and were generally professional standing troops, even elite troops. The tagmata (plural of tagma) were the direct descendants of the Imperial Guard units of the late Roman Empire.

Theotokos: an Eastern Orthodox title for the Virgin Mary, it literally translates to "God-Bearer" and serves as a reminder of her close maternal relationship with Jesus. There are three feast days associated with the Theotokos in the Eastern Orthodox church, but the one mentioned in Chapter 4 is November 21st, the Theotokos' Entrance into the Temple.

Þór: the Scandinavian god Thor

Throne of Solomon: a Byzantine appellation for the throne of the Eastern Roman Empire.

Trimaria: a fictional minor kingdom in the Aegis Rhōmaiōn, on the outskirts of the Empire. It corresponds roughly to the Crimean Peninsula in Ukraine.

Tylpt: a Scandinavian term meaning "dozens."

Útgarðr: another Scandinavian name for Jotunheim (unless Útgarðr was the capital of Jotunheim), the home of the frost giants and mountain giants. If Scandinavia was cold, Útgarðr was colder.

Valhalla: Odin's heaven, the great feasting-hall where Odin awaits Ragnarök with the Valkyries and the greatest of human warriors.

Varangian: one of the mercenary warriors of Scandinavian, Slavic, or Saxon ethnicity who served as the elite bodyguards of the Byzantine Emperor. The political situation in the Empire was so dangerous that it was safer to have mercenary bodyguards than to allow Byzantines whose loyalty might be to a rival to carry weapons near the emperor.

Ves heill: an often-raucous Old Norse toast, it literally means "be well" and is the source of the term "wassail."

Wergelðr: literally "man gold," the price someone who had caused the death or injury of someone else paid to the victim and/or his family in many northern European cultures. It served as an apology, compensation, and a reason to let the killer live.

Wifgelðr: literally "woman gold" or "wife gold," the price a man agreed to pay his wife if they become estranged due to some action on his part. While Viking-age Scandinavian women were generally in a strong position in a divorce, the term for this payment (and the fact that it would be in portable wealth) is one that I hypothesized using Viking-age Norse linguistic elements. Grimar's promised payment in Chapter 4 is intended to be hyperbolic, so he has every reason to always be a good husband to Ásaka.

Zatrikion: the form of chess played in the Byzantine Empire

A Note from the Author

Writing this book has been quite an adventure! After some friends requested a story for their reign in a medieval reenactment group, I had about two months to research two cultures I had only a passing knowledge of, outline a plot that would last for six months and relate in some way to the actual events of their reign, and get started writing so I could achieve my goal of posting the story in serial installments each week to my website and Facebook for everyone in the group to read.

As I researched the cultures and got to know the characters in the Saga, I realized that it wanted to be something much bigger than I'd planned – at least a thick stand-alone novel, probably a trilogy. And I'd have to change some things before I published the longer work, to place the work in its own world instead of one shaped by the reenactment group.

But in the meantime, many of the people who asked or agreed to be Tuckerized for the Saga have requested a nicely printed volume of the work they first read in serialized form. If you're reading this, either you're one of the wonderful people who helped me bring this book to life, you received the link from one of them or from my newsletter, or the algorithm decided to show it to you even though I'm not doing any marketing for this book. In any case, I appreciate your interest and sincerely hope that you'll enjoy both this volume and the full-grown work.

One final note: this entire work and the foundation work for the full series had been completed before Russia's invasion of Ukraine, which has been a separate nation with a distinct but related history for most of the time since its formation as an outer province in the Eastern Roman Empire. If my fictional tale of a land based on Ukraine can help draw the reader's attention to the real history of the nation, then I am greatly pleased even though raising Ukraine's visibility was never my primary goal in writing the Saga. Back when I started writing it, few people I spoke with seemed to know much about Ukraine, aside from the fact that it existed... somewhere.

I wish things could have stayed that way.

Acknowledgements

I couldn't have written this book without a lot of help and inspiration. Alex Cooley and April Cox provided the inspiration for this story and a lot of information about the type of conflicts and interactions that we wanted to see. Amy Cooley's friendship was and is inspiring.

And then there are all those wonderful people who didn't run away when I approached them about basing a character on them – or who approached me and *asked* to be included. While everyone mentioned here and many, many more will someday be represented in the larger work, I could only get a fraction of my volunteers into the first six chapters. And there are so many beautiful people who agreed to be included! There were people who have become Trimarian legends, like Kem Cason, Suellen Plonski, Daniel Fitzgerald, Linda Archer, Jeanne Stanley, Jonathan Sidwell, Robert Buchanan, Michael T. Moore, Mark Leggett, and J. P. Corwyn. Others, who enriched Trimaria with their presence, included Susan Kimball, Kevin Halleran, Cerric and Nathan Thomas, Christopher Lizon, Rick and Susan Allen, Doug McLean, Julio Devere, Janet and Ed Stapleton, Deborah Knight, Steve Beal, Vivienne Payne, Libby Peters Coutch, Lynn Tackett, Tracy H., and many, many others. The friends who joined us included Paul Snow and Raquelle Crotty. I won't name the children of Trimaris who helped to give this land its special spark of personality, but they and their parents know who they are.

The folk of the Writer Dojo have provided more information about indie publishing than I'd thought could be found in one source. You've made this part of the process easy. I can heartily recommend both the podcast and the Facebook group to any new, inexperienced, or would-be authors reading this.

For Further Reading

Haywood, John. *Northmen: The Viking Saga, AD 793-1241.* NY: Thomas Dunne Books, 2016.

Komnene, Anna. *The Alexiad.* Trans. NY: Penguin Classics, 2009.

Norwich, John Julius. *A Short History of Byzantium.* NY: Knopf, 1739.

Soth, Amelia. "The Marvelous Automata of Antiquity." JSTOR Daily. https://daily.jstor.org/the-marvelous-automata-of-antiquity/. June 7, 2018.

About the Author

Speculative fiction author Sophie G. Michaels was born in the rich rolling hills of Pennsylvania and lives in sunny central Florida when she's not being paid to travel. She loves the romance of the past as much as the possibilities of the future and strives to bring them both to life in her work.

Sophie writes most genres of speculative fiction, as well as historical poetry. Her published works include "Homecoming," "The Battle of Anderida Forest," "Return to Bethlehem," and *While Rivers Flow*. She can be found online at authorsophiegmichaels.substack.com and at SophieGMichaelsWrites.WordPress.com.

See me at
SophieGMichaelsWrite
s.WordPress.com!